Rejection to the Alpha King's Daughter

Rejection Series, Volume 3

Alana Dyer

Published by Alana Dyer, 2023.

Table of Contents

Chapter 1 - Once Upon A Time... As if!...1

Chapter 2 - A Destiny Set in Motion..2

Chapter 3 – The Outcast Princess 7

Chapter 4 - Training through the Years 12

Chapter 5 – Belle of the Ball 17

Chapter 6 - Princess Rogue 22

Chapter 7 - The White Spirit..28

Chapter 8 – Allies...34

Chapter 9 – A Breath of Freedom 40

Chapter 10 – Lessons 44

Chapter 11 – Bittersweet Decision 50

Chapter 12 – A Journey with New Friends 53

Chapter 13 – A Lawful Vampire...57

Chapter 14 – Temporary Home 64

Chapter 15 – Albot the Rogue 71

Chapter 16 – Trust...76

Chapter 17 - City Rogues..81

Chapter 18 – Moving Back to Wolf Country 87

Chapter 19 – Pack Astraea 93

Chapter 20 – A Hard Conversation...100

Chapter 21 – A Hidden Spy 107

Chapter 22 – Weeding out a Spy 111

Chapter 23 - Farewell, Astraea 118

Chapter 24 – Royal Pack 121

Chapter 25 – Royal Ball..126

Chapter 26 – Battle for the Throne 129

Chapter 27 – Narin's Truth...134

Chapter 28 – A Declaration of War...140

Chapter 29 – Realization...144

Chapter 30 - True Mates...147

Chapter 31 – Allies' Arrival 151

Chapter 32 – United 156

Chapter 33 - A Sense of Normalcy...160

Chapter 34 – The Dawn of War.. 162
Chapter 35 – The Final Battle 164
Chapter 36 – Coro's End 167
Chapter 37 – The Royal Family 171
Chapter 38 - A Date with Destiny.. 176
Chapter 39 – Soul Returns Home.. 179
Chapter 40 – A New Destiny Set in Motion.............................. 183

Dedication

This book is dedicated to all the people who have been used, cheated on, and hurt. Remember that Rejection is a new beginning!

Chapter 1 - Once Upon A Time... As if!

Do you know the stories of werewolves, beings that shift every full moon into mindless beasts with only the urge to hunt?

Well, what would you say if I told you that we exist, that werewolves exist and walk amongst you in the cities you live in?

What if I told you that the full moon is a myth created to protect our kind so that no human would go on a werewolf hunt because a Rogue or a Soulless attacked the innocents?

What if I told you hat I am the ruler of all wolves – The Alpha Queen – who keeps my kind safe and hidden from humans and hunters alike, who, with the help of witches, is able to put up barriers that only the supernaturals walking earth can see and go through?

I am Crystalline Thorn, the supposedly unwanted daughter to Alpha King Alexander, the daughter that was abused and rejected when the truth of me being a runt came out.

I am the she-wolf who survived a war and learned the truth of my heritage thanks to Amberle and Geminie.

I am the wolf that rules all wolves.

But I am getting ahead of myself. I should start from the beginning of my tale for you all to learn...

Chapter 2 - A Destiny Set in Motion

A distant time in past...

The King smiles as he looks down at his twin pups, Crystalline and Selene, in the flickering glow of the candlelight. His mate, Queen Luna, and his eldest, Prince Coro, looking on from a distance as Coro tries to get the attention of his exhausted mother. Luna had done a good job of giving birth to their pups, laboring from the moment the sun come up until the moon was high in the sky when the pups were born.

She had cause quite a stir with the maids in the stone walls of the palace when her water broke, the maids quickly helping Luna to the birthing chamber on the second floor. One had sent a guard to the training field where wolves sparred in metal armor or in wolf form to find King Spirit and inform him of his Queen's birth, while another navigated the cold corridors towards the Witch's tower to bring the midwife over.

King Spirit rushed to the palace after leaving his Beta in charge, making his way to the birthing chamber just in time to help the maids remove his wife's large ballgown from her body to allow her more movement. It was a long thirteen hours of laboring, but with the light of the full moon bathing their twin daughters and casting the same magic their mother possesses onto them the moment they were born, the King and Queen both knew instantly that their princesses would have a great destiny ahead of them.

"Who came first?" King Spirit asks, turning to look at the midwife, a witch named Cassandra. Her red as blood hair and eyes as blue as the sky are such a contrast to her true age; no one would think this woman is two hundred years old already. But the Witch is the reason the wolves can stay hidden from the hunters that wish to kill them.

"Selene did, Sire. She has the same Goddess powers as her mother," Cassandra responds, pointing to the firstborn daughter, whose little hair already reflected like a prism in the small glow of the candlelight.

"Crystalline came next and the power in her blood nearly suffocated me. It is stronger than the Prince," The witch continues, a smile on her face as she looks at the white-haired pup.

"Well then, Selene will take my place as the Moon Goddess when the time comes," Luna croaks weakly, a happy smile on her pale face.

"What about Crystalline?" Coro asks, looking at his newborn twin sisters with distain. The King frowns. He knows his son had been neglected the last six weeks with his mother's pregnancy coming to an end. But the King and Queen did their best to give Coro as much attention as they could while preparing him to become an older brother.

Coro pays no attention to Selene, already knowing that she will not be a bother to him with her inheriting their mother's legacy as the next Goddess. But Crystalline will be the *thorn* in his side when it comes to what he believes is his rightful place on the throne. The young pup can already feel the power of the Royal Blood flowing through her and could tell that she will surpass him in everything as soon as her training begins. He does not want to lose the throne he grew up being told will be his. He likes knowing that all the wolves listen to him, and he can freely torture those who disobey the six year old. All this will change if his sister is in the picture.

"Well, Coro, Crystalline and you will both train as leaders. One will become my heir and the other will become a Beta to their sibling or an Alpha of their own pack. Only time will tell," King Spirit answers him absentmindedly, not noticing the malicious look that the Prince sends to his sister. Witch Cassandra notices this however, realizing the smart Prince with connections across the supernatural realm may begin scheming despite his innocent-looking face.

Fearful for the twin daughters of her King and Queen, the Witch steps forward and reaches into her pouch, pulling out two silver necklaces with moonstone charms attached, happy to have made these protection charms for the twins in advance. She has treated many wolves the last year after they have been wrongfully punished by Prince Coro. Of course, the King and Queen could not believe their firstborn to be so malicious and chalked it up to being a rambunctious pup, but the Witch knew better. She knew one of the Princesses will be powerful and that the Prince would not like the competition. He already has it in his little mind that he owns the world, much to his parents' teachings.

"My King, with the help of some elves I was able to create protection charms for the Princesses. The moonstone that looks like the moon will be for Crystalline, as a reminder that her sister watches over her as the next Goddess. The moonstone shaped like a snowflake will remind Selene of her sister down on earth where the Royal Pack sits, and winter comes early," she says quietly, seeing the concern on her King's face.

"But the chains are silver. Silver harms us." He states with worry, the urge to throw those necklaces away instantly building inside of him. Cassandra smiles at him reassuringly before she gently places the necklaces around the twins' necks, much to her King and Queen's looks of protest. But shock fills the two royals as the silver causes no harm, and Coro looks on in rage. He always loved the colour silver, but the scar on his palm from touching a silver coin reminds him that he is incapable of holding the material.

The twins open their eyes, Selene's as white as the moon and Crystalline's as colourful as a light reflecting off a prism, and stare at the woman who has now handed them a gift. They already like her, their hands reaching out to grab the edge of her sleeves.

"As I said, their blood is strong. I have seen in a vision that both twins are immune to silver and their Destiny will be great. Silver can become their protection from those that wish to harm them." The witch chuckles, allowing the twins to cling to her sleeves. King Spirit nods, looking at his Queen who smiles at him.

"We will start to prepare silver jewelry and weapons for them then," The King states, walking over to pick up Selene and bring her to her mother before returning to hold Crystalline. With the King's promise, Cassandra bids her farewell to her rulers and takes her leave to allow the royal couple and Coro to bond with the twins. But worry still gnaws at her for Crystalline's safety. She has a feeling her destiny will be altered soon.

A week passes with Cassandra praying to the Goddess of Destiny Morai to protect the twins, as the feeling of something horrible happening soon grows. She spends her days either in her tower praying in the altar room to her chosen Deity for the safety of Crystalline and that the pup may live a good life, or with the Queen and the twins, always chanting a spell of protection over the two pups in hopes to keep them safe from Prince Coro.

Word of his cruelty to Crystalline has spread. Maids will find him holding Selene, bonding with her while Crystalline is left in the cradle, screaming for her needs to be taken care of. A maid will walk away for a moment to help with Selene only to find Crystalline missing and after a few minutes of searching, will find the princess outside in the cold night slowly freezing with Prince Coro's scent all over her. These incidents of cruelty towards Crystalline have reached the King and Queen's ears, making them more protective over the newborn pup and placing a harsher punishment on their eldest child. It is evident that the young Prince does not like his sister and has been plotting something dark and sinister.

On a dark, snowy night, Witch Cassandra put away her leather-bound notebooks after writing her observations for the day. She had just spent her day making sure the twin princesses are healthy and ready to be introduced to their nation now that they are a week old. She sighs, the feeling of unease growing inside her when she sets aside her quill and ink in their rightful spot on her desk before climbing the stairs to her altar at the top of the tower.

She flicks her fingers, lighting all of the candles around the statue of a child dressed in a modest gown, then carefully lowers herself to her knees and wraps a rosary made of rose quartz, amethyst, quartz crystal and blue lace agate around her hand before starting her prayers. She can feel a shift in the energy surrounding the palace and hopes that the prayers will dispel all the negativity she has felt throughout the day. Little does she know that Coro has planned something no one expected. While Cassandra continues her prayer to Goddess Morai, the feeling of something horrible about to happen grows, the air becoming heavy with negativity.

"Please, Goddess, keep Princess Crystalline safe." She whispers, a tear falling slowly down her face and onto the statue. She focuses hard, putting her magic into her prayer, hoping to reach her chosen deity.

As she prays, a guard rushes to her tower, fear and anger on his face. He opens the door on the first floor, realizing that the witch is not there as the urgency in his eyes deepens. He takes a deep breath, scenting the air in hopes of finding their only hope in fixing the situation the guards have found themselves in, and feels relieved to learn that the witch is up in her prayer room.

Without hesitation, he climbs the stairs in a rush, taking the stone steps two at a time in hope of making it to Cassandra quickly. Finally, the landing comes into view and he reaches for the handle. Bursting through the door and allowing a cold rush of air to extinguish all the candles except the red infused with the power of the sun and moon and used to pray to the Goddess of Destiny, the guard huffs and puffs, gasping for breath, fighting to get the words out.

"What is so urgent that you have to interrupt my prayers?" Cassandra asks furiously, looking over at the guard who stares at her with hope in his fearful gaze.

"Princess Crystalline is missing. We need your help to find her, Witch Cassandra!"

Chapter 3 – The Outcast Princess

"Crystalline, you are uselessly slow. Why is it so hard for you to be faster?!" My father growls out in frustration as I cross the finish line of the track in the training building for the umpteenth time tonight. Leaning against a pillar for support, I try my best to catch my breath and look at the clock on the wall. Shocked to see it reads ten thirty at night, I internally groan, realizing it has been three hours since father made me run laps inside instead of letting me join the others in hand-to-hand combat outside in the winter snow.

"Father, I am trying my best, but it's been three hours. I am exhausted and need a break to be able to go faster." I plead, hoping to reason with the mountain of a man before me. All he does is growl, his anger radiating off him and towards me, but I stand my ground as the chain with the moonstone orb sways slightly from my neck. Being the only child and without any sons, Alexander has forced me to train for years on end to be a strong heir to the throne, always forcing me to run laps at night and fight wolves in the day knowing I am unable to shift. He thinks tough love is all I need to be a perfect heir, but this treatment only makes my hatred and resentment towards him grow stronger. The need to run away and never look back is something I contemplate almost everyday.

"Don't you dare talk back to me, Crystalline! It is unbefitting of a Princess!" A hand connects to the left side of my face, sending me to the rubber floor of the track field as the pain radiates across of my face. Holding my hand to my cheek in hopes to stop the stinging, I keep my head down as Alexander begins to rant about my purpose in life. I have to find a proper mate and produce proper male heirs, heirs he always wanted but instead became stuck with me. To him, I should be just like his whores he sleeps with, seen but not heard, strong but submissive.

"You are a disgrace, but the only heir I have. Had you not gotten your mother killed, and given my inability to get anyone else pregnant, you would have been sold to some Alpha long ago already." He scoffs. I want to yell back, to fight and argue that had he not been fucking that pack whore, he would have been in the family room with mother and I watching the movie when the Rogues attacked. He would have been on time to protect my mother and stop that Rogue from ripping her throat out. Instead, the guard showed up just in time to stop the Rogue from killing me. I keep my head down, waiting for his rant to end as usual, for his anger to dissipate.

"You're an outcast amongst this pack, and no one likes you. If you weren't my daughter, you would have been thrown out long ago. Sadly, I need you to continue the bloodline." His words sting, but I am used to this verbal abuse, used to him cursing me and my existence and him belittling me in front of everyone. I just hope he leaves soon so that I can run and hide away in the forest for a while.

One thing is for sure though, because of my father's disdain for me and outright verbal abuse, I became the outcast Princess. No one likes me, they only tolerate me due to the ability to produce an heir. If it weren't for my bloodline, I know I would end up like the Omegas in the pack, abused and raped with no one to care about whether they live or die. I hate my father for this, hate how the pack has slowly declined in strength due to his ruling. He cares more for chasing after pack whores than training his wolves, more for trying to produce a male heir than to actually be a proper father to me. He is toxic to the Thorn line – toxic to the Royal Pack – and I have a feeling our ancestor King Coro would disapprove of him.

With a final look of distain, my father turns away in a huff and walks out, leaving me alone to catch my breath. Rolling onto my back, I stare up at the moon roof in the ceiling, the full moon shining down on me. Closing my eyes and wrapping my hands around the moonstone orb on the silver chain, I think of my mother, of joining her in the Goddess's realm and ending the misery that is my life. She would be disappointed in me, though. Her final words to live and fight for my life always echo in my mind when I feel like giving up. I know that even if I want to join her, I can't. One day, I will become Queen, and when that day comes, I have to make sure that what happened to her never happens to anyone in this pack again.

With a sigh, I slowly climb to my feet and walk towards the closest wall of the training building before making my way towards the door facing the direction of the northern peaks. My body is exhausted from running nonstop, my legs tired and sore from overuse, forcing me to use the walls for support until my healing power kicks in. I want to be deep in the forest, alone in the cold snow. One day, this pack will realize that they needed me more than they thought, and my father will regret the way he has treated me. But right now, I need to focus on living like my mother would have wanted me to.

Stepping out of the training building, the bitter winter wind hits me first, making me shiver but invigorating me to keep walking. The forest is my safety, the snow a reminder to keep fighting to stay alive. Walking deeper, I feel the pain in my body lessen, each step becoming steadier until I no longer need the support of the trees to keep moving. But my journey is short when I come across the river I like to sit beside, the water surprisingly warm due to the hot springs it flows from.

Taking a seat by the water's edge on a patch of green grass unaffected by the cold weather, I quickly remove my shoes and dip my feet into the flowing warm water, relishing in the warmth that travels through me and soothes the aches from running for long periods of time.

"Hey, Crysta!" A voice calls out. I smile, turning my head in the direction of the call just in time to see my friend Matrix walking out from the tree line towards me, the guard-in-training giving me one of his famous easygoing smiles.

"Hey, Trix." I call back, watching as the fifteen year old takes a seat beside me and pulls out his Swiss Army knife from his pocket to whittle away at a piece of pine wood that he picked up from the tree line before joining me.

"What brings you out here?" I ask, watching his hands work away at the wood. The warmth from the river prevents me from feeling the bitter cold of the winter, the grass I sit on still releasing its fresh scent that calms me down.

"Nothing really. I seen you exit the training grounds and thought you would like some company." His answer has me smiling as a comfortable silence settles between us with only the sounds of his knife scraping away at the wood. My best friend always knows what I need when I needed something, and right now his silent company is definitely what I need. I turn away from watching the wood in his hand change forms to look at the changing sky above me. I lean back on my hands and focus on the stars, wondering if I will be one of them one day. And then I see it.

Shooting across the sky in a brilliant silver light is a shooting star, the star twinkling and dancing in the dark indigo sky, with a tail trailing behind it like fairy dust left in its wake. Closing my eyes, I make a silent wish, wishing my life will change for the better. It's stupid, but right now I can use a bit of magic, even if it is in the form of a simple wish.

Opening my eyes just in time to see the star disappear, I smile, turning to Matrix, wanting to go back to the palace and get some sleep as tomorrow will be a long day. That is when I feel it.

Pain like hundreds of knives heated to a thousand degrees stabs through me, wreaking havoc on my body. My mouth opens in a silent scream as I curl into myself, tears streaming down my face with me being unable to form any words. It feels like death is consuming me, but I want to fight it. I can't die yet at only thirteen years old.

"Crystalline!" Matrix calls out, dropping the wood and knife to cradle my body. His worried gaze searches my face for any answer before moving to my body. I watch as his face goes from tense with worry to soft with relief as he lets out a chuckle. This idiot has the gall to laugh while I am in pain.

"Try to take a deep breath, Crysta. The pain is you shifting for the first time." He reassures me, running fingers through my hair as he coaches me into breathing slowly. The pain lessens, but I am still left curled into a ball feeling like death is clawing at me, ready to take me away.

"Breathe, Crysta! You just have to let the shift happen. Fighting it will only kill you." Matrix advises. I whimper wondering what he expects me to do while my insides feel like they are being ripped apart by burning claws. I want to keep fighting this pain, to prevent it from hurting me but his reminder that fighting will kill me causes me to close my eyes and focus on breathing.

I feel my bones snapping, my breath catching in my throat as the pain causes me to scream. I feel pin pricks through my skin as something grows out excruciatingly slow. My face elongates, my jaw snapping without warning, causing my scream to turn into a gurgling mix between a howl and a whimper.

Finally, the pain eases its deathlike grip on me and my breath comes easily. My body feels heightened, the scents in the air stronger. I sneeze from the overwhelming scent of pine, rubbing my nose with my paw.

"Crystalline!" Matrix gasps forcing me to open my prismatic eyes to stare at him with confusion.

"You... You are a white wolf." My tail thumps happily. A white wolf is rare, only reserved for those with royal blood line. It means we are closely related to Alpha Spirit, the first Alpha King.

"You don't get it, Crystalline. You're a white runt!" Worry and fear is evident in his voice as the seriousness of the situation settles. A runt is the worst thing anyone can be in the Royal Pack. It is cause for instant banishment if not death, depending on if the runt in question is male or female. Runts are only good for one thing in my fathers eyes – being bred to produce strong pups or sold to form alliances.

My father will kill me if he finds out that his so-called useless daughter is a runt. That or he will wait for my first heat and breed me with a wolf he chooses for a true heir.

Chapter 4 - Training through the Years

Fourteen Years Old:

I growl in frustration as my small frame falls into a snow drift, hating this training exercise while I dodge trees in wolf form with my white fur blending into the snow perfectly. My body is only three feet tall in wolf form, my head barely able to see over a standard white picket fence. But Matrix insisted on me training in this form in the forest. Matrix is a pro at tracking and hunting, the sixteen year old already tracking wolves for days even though he is a Warrior. With a nose like his, so strong that he can smell a Soulless before it can even cross the pack line, it takes everything in me to stay ahead of my friend.

Matrix has unfortunately made it his mission to train my speed and agility, something a runt like me could only inherit. Speed and agility will help me take down an enemy. Speed and agility will help protect myself, especially since father has made it his mission to make me seem weak in this pack. With speed and agility, I can take down my enemies and prove to be a strong Alpha Queen.

A yelp escapes my muzzle as I feel my paws slipping out from under me as a five-foot-six brown wolf tackles my small form. I can't help the sigh that escapes my lips as I stare at my friend who gives me a wolfish grin.

[You're easy to take down when distracted.] Matrix chuckles through our link, nuzzling me gently before licking my snout. I knew if a wolf could blush, I would be beet red right now.

[Sorry. But I will do better, I promise.] For some reason, I did not want to disappoint Matrix. He is my rock, the only person who knows I am a runt.

Sixteen Years Old:

The rush of wind through my fur has me excited for the first hunt. Matrix has been promising me this for over three years since I first shifted. I just turned sixteen today and the adrenaline of hunting my first kill deep in the forest is something I had dreamt of since I was a pup, when my mother first explained to me that eligible wolves can go for their first hunt and prove themselves to our pack. Of course, Father insisted I am too weak to go., claiming that only the strong should be allowed to go for their first hunt.

But Matrix as always stood up for me, stating my achievements in training, how I took down a group of Soulless while we were on the outskirts of the pack training my speed and agility, and how on the training grounds I can take down even the best of our Warriors. This and with the convincing of others stating that at thirteen I was the youngest in the pack to survive a first shift, and that joining the first hunt will help make me stronger and in turn provide strong pups to help rule the werewolf nation, my father was forced to finally agree to let me go for the first hunt.

[So, Crysta, do you want a blanket made of bear fur?] Trix asks with a laugh. I smirk, thinking of the pride hunting a bear comes with within the pack. Only Warriors and the strongest hunt bears. If I can bag one on my own, then respect will follow. Pack mates will understand that I am not as weak as father proclaims me to be, that I can hold my own against anyone.

[Yes. A bear will put that asshole and any other misogynistic wolf in their place for calling me weak. I am not a weak wolf!] I answer, a rumble of approval coming from my friend before we head off in the direction of bear country in neutral territory. Our aim is for seasoned bears that have lived long lives with expert fighting skills, ones without cubs. And I can't wait to have that damned blanket as proof that I am not the weakest in this pack. They will learn to respect me as their future Queen or be beaten into submission.

Our journey through neutral territory takes four days in wolf form and leads us closer to the Alaskan borders where bears are easily found. I can smell other wolves, some from the royal pack, others from allied packs. All are here to join their first hunt.

[Should we shift into human form?] I am unsure whether or not it will be safe.

[No. I have a few friends from allied packs coming to join us. They know you are a runt but accept you as our future Queen.] Matrix answers, his brown wolf moving in front of my body and blocking me from view. I peer over his shoulder, spotting three wolves walking towards us, each with their head lowered in submission.

[Open your link, Crysta.] Matrix calls out. I sigh, closing my eyes and focusing on the link, allowing my mind to reach forward toward the three wolves whose stares are focused on my hidden body. I feel three pops in my mind, wincing when I connect to the three new wolves.

[Hello?] I call out tentatively.

[Hello, Princess.] A she-wolf replies, the middle of the three wolves stepping forward as her tail wags.

[I am Seria of the Harvest Willow, the other two are my cousins from the same back.] Seria introduces herself, the brown and tan wolf smiling at me. I am shocked to notice that she too is a runt, her wolf form smaller than me. I like her instantly, walking forward to rub my cheek against hers.

[It's nice to meet you all.] I say cheerily, happy to have other wolves around. With introductions finished, we all form a plan, one that involves all five of us battling a bear and bringing home a bear pelt.

Seventeen years old:

I groan as I land in the dust of the training field, laughter from the male I am fighting in front of me causing my anger to flare. He can laugh now, but I will gladly take this beating until I can figure out his skills. I watch as he turns his back on me, his movement becoming sloppy as he cockily gloats to his friends. I bet gloating about putting the "weak little Princess" on her ass is something to be proud about in this pack, but not for long.

Silently climbing to my feet, I creep towards the male who is already making plans on how to spend the money he "won" from the bets. Odds are against me as I am the only female training with the Warriors. The males think I am weak thanks to my father's propaganda against me all these years. But Matrix and I knew better. I will have the win and take all the money with Matrix.

With a grin, I stay in Narin's blind spot. He may be my future Beta as per the heritage rule, but I will be Queen and his future Alpha. He will learn to show me respect today and know he is not better than me. Before he can sense me and while the others were already celebrating his win, I kick his feet out from beneath him and watch as he falls to the ground with a shrill shriek.

While silence reigns over the training field, I quickly straddle the twenty year old wolf's torso and send a quick open palm thrust to his nose. A sickening crunch echoes in the quiet room, with blood gushing from the broken nose I had just given Narin. He tries to fight me off, but I send a quick punch to his jaw with another crunch sounding upon connection with my fist.

I am quickly thrown off of him as he lets his anger take control and releases a deafening snarl. Quickly rolling into a somersault upon landing, I stand to my feet gracefully and prepare my stance for a fight. An opponent clouded by anger is easy to defeat.

"You bitch!" Narin roars, his anger-filled green eyes directed at me. I smirk, waving my hand in a *come hither* motion and waiting for his attack. This seems to have pissed him off further as he rushes me, his nails already turned into claws. Happy for the agility training that Matrix drilled into my brain, I dodge each swipe directed towards me, always one step ahead of Narin as I toy with him, laughing gleefully with each swipe he fails to land. Of course, every so often I step in range just to inflict my own damage. I quickly jab here and land a kick or two there, and Narin soon resembles a dishevelled madman sporting a bloodied and bruised face.

Bored of this cat and mouse chase, I dodge one final punch from Narin and use my momentum to send a roundhouse kick to his torso, hearing the crunch of more bones when my foot connects. Without losing stride, I send a punch to his shoulder, hard enough to inflict damage but not break any bones. He has enough bones to heal and will be out of commission for quite some time. Watching as he falls to his knees, I grab his hair, preventing this Beta wolf from falling further, and smirk.

"Check mate." I state triumphantly, releasing my grip on his locks and allow his fall to continue. His eyes hold fear before the pain of the match renders him unconscious. I just proved to all watching that I, Crystalline Thorn and future Queen, am not weak.

"Trix, you prick, you owe me fifty percent of the money!" I call out, making my way to my best friend and fist bumping him in triumph.

"You know what, it's worth it seeing how all these high and mighty macho guys now fear you." He laughs, ruffling my hair. I turn and smirk at the now silent crowd. Of course their expectations of me were low. Now, they hold both fear and respect after taking down the strongest Warrior in the pack.

"Someone help my future Beta to the medical ward." I bark out the order, seeing the crowd standing there unmoving.

"And as soon as he is healed, make sure his training is increased. We can't have a weak Beta in this pack." I continue, leaning against Matrix as he counts the money earned, happy that he and I made a bet for my victory as we had made a killing off of these idiotic wolves.

"Yes, Alpha!" They shout in unison, some rushing to take Narin away on a stretcher while others slowly spread out around the training room to begin their own sparring. I have a feeling that what happened here will soon be spread amongst the pack.

"I almost forgot. Here is your necklace back." Matrix chuckles, his eyes soft as he looks at me. I smile as Matrix helps to place my silver chain with the moonstone orb around my neck. I am happy he kept it safe for me while Narin and I fought.

The two of us decide that we have trained enough for the day as he places his hand on the small of my back and we make our way to our usual river spot. We both could use some peace and quiet.

Chapter 5 – Belle of the Ball

Glaring at the ballgown hanging from the wall, I think about what will happen today and why my father is forcing me to wear it. Today is the celebration of a new Alliance. Future Goddess Geminie offered an alliance with my father earlier this year and negotiations finally went through. As such, Father announced this to all the packs in the world with happiness and even planned a ball of honor with packs such as Blood Moon of North America, Hauringu Uindo from Japan. La Chasse from France, and Silver Hounds from England, the strongest packs in the world.

Unfortunately for me, this meant that I would have to shift into my wolf form to howl with Goddess Geminie at the full moon to complete the ceremony. Even worse, this means my secret of being a runt will be revealed and could lead to one of three fates.

Fate number one, Father imprisons me to become a brood mare and produce strong pups to continue to royal bloodline with my mate.

Fate number two, I am disowned from the pack and become a Rogue.

Fate number three, my execution would be right on the spot. I prefer the second fate as turning Rogue meant I have a chance to train and fight for my throne back. Seeing how Father never liked runts and always shipped them off to a pack that will treat them as nothing more than slaves, I have a feeling he may choose the first option and sell any of my pups that are runts to the highest bidder for power.

"Princess Crystalline?" My Maid Hanna calls out as she steps into my room.

"I'm still here." I chuckle out, seeing her remove the protective gloves from her hand. No one can enter my room without them, the silver on the door knobs preventing any from entering my room without being burned by the pure silver.

"Thank the Goddess for that. It is time to dress you for the ball." She sighs with relief, seeing me in front of said dress with my bear fur blanket draped around my shoulders for warmth and comfort for what is to come. Turning to the maid, I give her a sad smile as she places the glove on a side table and wraps me in her arms in a hug I desperately needed.

"Happy birthday, Princess. I know it's not the day you wanted, but you are so strong. Just know the maids have your back and there is a surprise from us for later tonight." I smile, thanking her for her support and birthday wish before we both turn back to the ballgown hanging on the wall.

A white, strapless, corseted gown with lace applique. It is ironic, considering I am a white runt trapped by the societal norms my father created. I will be a white runt in a white dress ready to be exposed.

Hanna takes my bear fur blanket from me carefully, draping it over the nearby sofa before helping me into the gown. She is careful with helping me step into the gown so as not to ruin my hair or makeup. Only my shift can ruin my perfectly made-up look as I have to portray the look of a perfect royal doll to the guests.

Her praises of how beautiful I am and how the light nude eyeshadow placed perfectly on my eyelids brings out the multiple colours swirling in my iris, remind me of the fact that I am different. Only those with a strong bloodline can poses the prismatic eyes.

With my dress pulled up and Hanna tightening the corset to where I can barely breath, let alone eat if I wanted to, I am turned to the mirror looking like the perfect doll with a sad smile. I worry for what will happen tonight. Hanna rushes into my closet, most likely to bring the finishing touches of my outfit, and I wait silently for her to return.

"Crysta, its me!" The sound of the door opening and closing followed by Matrix walking in makes me smile. At twenty, Matrix worked his way up the totem pole of ranks and soon became the Theta-in-training. When I take the throne, this wolf with Alpha blood will become my third in command.

His blond hair that is usually in a haphazard mess is now combed back and held down with gel, his tailored black suit doing little to hide the muscles underneath from years of training. It is the first time I have seen him today, and the hope of him being my mate is soon dashed when no sparks are ignited along my skin nor does his scent drive me crazy. I do my best to hide my disappointment, my one hope of the wolf who cares for me the most being my mate and co-ruler dashed. I will just have to search for my mate the old-fashioned way now.

"Happy birthday." He smiles at me, pulling away from the hug as he looks my body up and down, a hint of lust in his eyes. I can tell that the lack of mate sparks disappointed him as well. I know he wants me the same way I want him, the topics of us being possible mates always one we discuss since his eighteenth birthday two years ago. It sadly is just not meant to be.

"Theta Matrix, care to help put the silver tiara on our Princess?" Hanna's voice cuts through the silence as she approaches us, her carefully balancing the tiara on the pillow so as not to be burned by the pure silver. I chuckle as I realize she forgot to put on her gloves again.

"Of course, considering I am the only one who can touch it other than Crystalline and the Goddess." He answers, deftly picking up the tiara encrusted with diamonds and moonstones and gently placing the delicate jewelry atop my head without ruining my hairstyle, a bun with delicate curls and bangs swept to the left side.

"Perfect! Now off you two go before the Alpha King blows a gasket." Hanna states, shooing Matrix and I out of the room with a smile. The walk is long with the click, click, click sounds of my heels on the stone floor. With Matrix soon seven feet ahead of me due to his long strides, I find myself struggling to keep up.

"You okay, Crysta?" My friend asks, turning to find me leaning on the wall trying to catch my breath.

"Yep. Just a heavy ballgown and heels makes it hard to keep up." I answer, glaring down at my gown. He chuckles, striding back towards me and scooping me into his arms.

"What are you doing!" I squeal, quickly wrapping my arms around his neck so that I do not fall.

"Taking you to the ball room. If we are late, your father will kill me and punish you." He chuckles. The way to the ball becomes much quicker as Matrix comfortably caries me through the corridors in peaceful silence. There are no words to say between us as the hope we both felt wanting to be each other's mates is diminished without mercy. His pine and fresh water scent wraps around me, comforting me while also fueling my disappointment.

Why couldn't the Moon Goddess pair us together? Matrix is Alpha blooded, so he would have made a great Alpha King.

Keeping my thoughts to myself, I close my eyes to settle my emotions. I can't let my father or anyone else see my turmoil and deem me hysterical and weak in front of the guests. As we grow closer to the double doors closed with the barest sounds of music coming forward, I open my eyes and find myself being gently placed on my feet moments before King Alexander comes into view, his own entourage including his Beta, Mikael, and the future Beta, Narin.

Curtsying to my father, I catch a whiff of something delectable, peppermint and chocolate, and know at once my mate is near. If it's not Matrix, then they are in attendance tonight.

"Silver as always, I see." King Alexander states with dissatisfaction, his hatred towards me evident in his eyes. He hates that only I inherited the immunity of silver, while he cannot touch it without burning his skin. I keep my face a mask of calm, not wanting to cause a commotion today with what awaits me later.

Silver is the kryptonite of wolves, a metal used to kill us during the witch hunts for many years and is still used to this day by Hunters. After my mother watched in horror the night I found the moonstone necklace in the middle of a moonflower meadow and placed the silver chain around my neck, she realized that the metal did not harm me like it did other wolves.

Right away everything from my jewelry to the metal embellishments on my doors were changed to pure silver, as a way to keep me safe and out of harm's way. A silver dagger was then gifted to me and I was enrolled into self-defence training as soon as possible.

"Father, silver is a way to protect me. As the only heir our bloodline will end if something happens to me, and the Goddess' line will take over as the next royals." I remind him, watching his jaw clench with irritation. The thought of our bloodline being replaced by distant relatives infuriates him more than the thought of me wearing silver.

His irritation amuses me as he and I take the lead in standing before the doors. Matrix is behind me, his presence bringing me peace with having to deal with my father and the consequences of what will come after my shift. I pray to my ancestors and the Moon Goddesses that tonight will go smooth as the doors open.

"Presenting his Majesty King Alexander Theon Thorn, and Her Highness Princess Crystalline Evangeline Thorn."

Chapter 6 - Princess Rogue

Walking into the ballroom with my father slightly ahead, I scan the crowd of fancily dressed dignitaries from around the globe. Werewolves stare back at us, bowing or curtsying to us, their King and Princess, and I internally roll my eyes. Sadly, today their respect for me will be gone. A runt that rules the werewolf world is not the ideal future ruler.

My eyes scan the room until I find who I am looking for, Geminie Starlight, my distant cousin and next heir to the throne, with her mate Ariven and daughter Destiny. Walking down the elegant steps, I make my way to where she stands as a light catches the necklace she is wearing: a snowflake-shaped moonstone. Her prism-coloured hair shifting colours as she moves and her moon-white eyes with a slightly grey pupil are the opposite of my white hair and prismatic eyes. Smiling, the future Goddess nuzzles her cheek against mine.

"A pleasure to finally meet you, Cousin." I speak first, pulling away to address the strong she-wolf before me.

"The pleasure is mine, Cousin." She smiles mischievously at me before turning to wink at Amberle who stands beside her own mate and twin daughters. The fiery red-headed wolf is holding onto an equally red-headed pup in her arms while her mate, Alpha Dominic, is guarding her protectively. Her words seem to hold some meaning between the two, and instinct tells me to trust the alpha wolves.

Catching my father's look of irritation, I decide to focus on the ceremony first, and later I can speak to the two she-wolves. Stepping back, I turn to the wolves in attendance and plaster on the well-practiced smile. It's show time, and I need to play the part of the perfect daughter in order to not anger my father.

"Welcome dignified guests, to the Alliance Ball." I state, bowing my head to the Alphas, Lunas and high-ranking wolves that have gathered here today.

"Today we welcome my cousin, Goddess Geminie and Alpha of Silver Crystal Crescent to the Royal Pack in hopes of the two packs forming and Alliance." Continuing, I once more turn to my cousin, my dress fanning out in a display of elegance, the fabric hanging to the curves of my body that seem to gain the approval of the unmated males in the room. I am nothing but a show for them, placed on display by my father.

"As such, I would like to invite Alpha Geminie to the moon dais to shift and howl as one before the Alliance Oath is uttered." Holding out my hand to the powerful she-wolf, I wait patiently for her to take it. She smiles at me, her delicate hand adorned in silver rings like my own is pressed to my skin.

"I see you are not the only one immune to silver," She chuckles and I smile back in amusement.

"It's a trait in the royal family I suppose. But we do have one exception." I retort smiling, looking back towards Matrix who sends me an encouraging smile.

"Your mate?" Geminie asks, looking between Matrix and me.

"No, my best friend. He can touch silver as well. No one knows why." I answer, turning back to look at my cousin.

"I can tell you why. His blood holds a hint of royal in it. I would say he is part of a bastard line." Shocked, I look back to Matrix trying to find any trace of the royal power in him, but I find nothing. I will have to look into it further when I have the time, but for not I have a ceremony to finish.

With our conversation done, we walk towards the dais, hand in hand until we are stopped by two maids. A robe of pure silver is draped onto our shoulders while the two maids wear protective gear and help us to undo the corseted dresses we wore today. Once free from our dresses and heels, the two of us make our way to the center of the moon dais.

[Matrix?] I call out nervously through our link waiting for the que to shift from the woman across from me.

[Here, Crystalline. The moment things go wrong I will be there to whisk you away. I asked Hanna to pack a few bags with clothes and cash for us if things go south. Yes, this includes your bear fur blanket.] He reassures me, his deep voice calming my nerves. Looking to Geminie, I see her smile at me as she gives a small nod, the signal to shift. Taking a deep breath, I close my eyes and allow the fear and nerves to melt away.

What ever happens tonight is destined my Goddess Morai. I just have to accept whatever fate I have coming to me. The sounds of bones breaking and merging into the shape of my wolf and my hair recedes as fur takes its place. Finally, under the silver cloak, I stand tall and proud, looking at the future Moon Goddess staring at me in surprise as her wolf towers over me by at least a foot and a half.

Gasps fill the silent room and all eyes stare at me. I am the runt with a silver tiara still atop of her head and the moonstone attached to the silver chain around her body.

"You filthy bitch!" An angry roar sounds from where my father sat on the throne. I know it is only a matter of minutes before he is in front of me. Turning, I brace myself just in time to feel his foot connect with my body, sending me sprawling to the floor. I can already tell I have a few broken ribs from the kick. Geminie quickly steps between us, snarling at my father. Ariven hands their child to Amberle before joining his mate in standing between my father and me.

"You are a runt, a filthy runt!" He screams, not daring to walk forward towards an angry Goddess who harnesses powers that could kill, and her overprotective mate ready to kill for his loved one blocking his way.

"That is no way to treat your daughter!" Ariven states, anger radiating in his voice.

"Who are you to tell me how to treat that bitch!" Father roars back.

"A father of a daughter myself. Daughters should be cherished, not beaten," Ariven roars back. I slowly climb to my feet and join the two, snarling at my father as he goes to take a step towards Ariven threateningly.

"Your Majesty, wait!" A shout in the crowd has the man before me stopping in his track. Annoyance and irritation at the person who prevented him from attacking me again. My ears are focused for that voice, my heart beating faster as something inside my mind begs me to find the owner. The delectable scent from earlier is stronger as the person that shouted draws closer.

"What is it, Narin?" My father demands, striding off of the dais and towards the future Beta.

"Crystalline. She is my mate." He answers, a look of disgust as if he has eaten something foul filling his handsome face. I want to make him smile. to have him look at me with love and not disgust in those green eyes of his, and I realize this is the mate bond making me want him.

"I'm sorry, Crystalline. But you're weak and a runt, and the pack can't have you ruling." He continues, turning his gaze towards me. I flinch at the hatred he shows, not understanding how he could look at his mate... at me like that. Wolves from Silver Crystal Crescent and Blood Moon circle the dais, blocking Alexander and Narin from reaching me with Amberle, Dominic and the three children joining us.

"Don't do what you plan to do, Narin." Amberle growls while Geminie is helped into a simple black dress, different from the blue ballgown she wore earlier.

"Amberle is right. You will regret this." The Future Moon Goddess states.

"Why shouldn't I? I don't need a runt for a mate." He chuckles out as a response. Angry, I shift into my skin form to feel a presence behind me and a shirt placed over my head. Taking in Matrix's scent, I quickly pull on the shirt and turn to glare at my mate.

"Do you plan to reject me, Narin? Is that what the two Alphas are warning you against?" I ask, seeing him smirk.

"What else is there that they can warn me about, Crystalline." A statement and not a question is his response. Angry, I take a deep breath and reach for my necklace to help ground me and calm my emotions before I say anything I may regret.

"Because we are mates, soulmates, Narin. We are meant to rule together." The crowd watches on with silence, their heads moving back and forth. The King and his men on one side, the Princess and two strong she-wolves on the other. My heart feels like it is breaking as the guests get to enjoy the drama unfolding, and I silently wish to gouge their eyes out.

"You are weak and worthless, Crystalline. I don't need a weak mate!" He snaps back, the anger radiating him forcing me to recoil in shock.

"Have you forgotten the many times I sent you to the infirmary just sparring in skin? Or the times I kicked your ass with my bare human fists while you were in wolf form?" I shout, fighting back the tears threatening to spill. A hand is placed on my shoulder, comforting me as I deal with my idiot of a mate.

"You're just spreading lies!" Narin shrieks, shaking as if I am spouting nonsense. Fine, if he wants to play this game then so can I. With eyes glowing, I direct my voice and allow the Royal command to leave my lips.

"Narin, by the power of the Royal Blood, I order you to tell the truth of whether or not I am weak!" His body goes rigid, his eyes blank as my command takes over. I wince, the mate bond throbbing with pain from commanding my mate, forcing me to take a deep breath.

"Due to training with the Princess, I have been sent to the hospital wing ten times both in human and wolf form." His voice is robotic and I smile, allowing the command to release my mate and watch as his rigid body drops to the floor. I can command the truth from him at a cost to the mate bond, but I cannot stop him from rejecting me. Murmurs amongst the crowd sound about the harsh treatment from my father and the rejection that is soon to follow.

"Damn it, Crystalline. I am so tired of you, the runt and outcast of the pack and the unloved daughter of the King!" Narin exclaims in anger as soon as he regains control of his body. I roll my eyes at his outburst, feeling Matrix move closer to me, his body just inches from mine. If only he had been my mate, we wouldn't be going through this situation.

"I, Narin Malkaric and future Beta of the Royal Pack reject you Princess Crystalline Thorn as my soulmate and break any bond that ties us together." He shouts in rage, standing protectively in front of my father while glaring at me. My heart shatters as a stabbing pain rips through me. My mate just rejected me in front of all to see.

"And I, Alpha King Alexander Thorn reject you, Crystalline Thorn from the Royal Pack turning you Rogue. You are no longer my child nor my heir." I screamed as soon as my father's words are uttered, the pain of the pack link being ripped from my body, severed like a head on the guillotine is so unbearable, worse than the rejection, that I wish death would take me right now. Strong arms wrapping around me keep me upright and from falling on my face.

"Matrix, leave that Rogue alone!" Alexander orders but I feel familiar arms tighten around me.

"No! My loyalty lies with Princess Crystalline!" Matrix retorts, his anger radiating in his words.

"Are you stupid? You'll lose everything, a pack, your family, even your Theta status!" Narin's voice pierces through the air. The chest that keeps me steady rumbles with laughter as I am scooped into the arms of my best friend, his hand keeping my face hidden in his chest.

"I'd rather become a rogue and train with Crystalline. As one of the few royals left, she will come back and take the throne. You never deserved to be King, Alexander. You're nothing but a sterile man whore." Sterile. Alexander is sterile. I try to keep this information while breathing through the stabbing pain, trying to keep myself conscious while blackness fades in and out. The pain of being rejected then turned Rogue forcibly is one that can kill any wolf, weak or strong.

"Let them leave. Tonight is a night of Alliance with the Future Moon Goddess." His voice is muffled by the throbbing headache that threatens to knock me unconscious, but Alexander is being merciful for now.

"Like I'd continue an alliance with you!" A female voice scoffs.

"Consider Silver Crystal Crescent and the allies of my pack your enemy, Alexander. I do not accept you as my King nor as an ally." I feel my body being carried away after those words, a powerful boom alerting me to an explosion. But the pain keeps clawing at me, the darkness inviting me to fade away and stop the pain from continuing to hurt me.

"Hang on, Crystalline, we are getting you out here." Matrix whispers, his voice the last thing I hear before the world around me goes black.

Chapter 7 - The White Spirit

"Geminie, we can't keep her here at the temple. The moonstone is proof enough that she is indeed the lost Princess." Muffled voices reach my ears, bringing me out of the darkness.

"What do you mean? I grew up with Crysta." Matrix exclaims, he seems confused.

"What Amberle means is that I am the daughter of the Current Moon Goddess. Crystalline is the daughter of the first Moon Goddess." I wish for those speaking to be silent. The pain is just too much to bear, and being woken when I should be healing is not a nice feeling.

"Shit, why is it glowing?" Someone exclaims. Glowing? What's glowing?

"She is being summoned by someone. My stone glows when one of the Goddesses want to talk to ..."

•••

A soft breeze caresses my skin, the scent of moonflowers reaching my nose and bringing me from the darkness that consumes me.

"I am happy to see you are awake." A man's voice from my right calls out, forcing me to jump in fright and turn. Standing on a hill, a tall six-foot-five male with white hair stares down at the forest before us, before he turns to me with a warm smile. Confused, I climb to my feet, wary of the man dressed in an outfit I can only describe as antique, something someone from the medieval period would wear.

"Who are you?" I ask, backing away and putting some distance between the man and me.

"I go by many names." He answers mysteriously, a hint of a smirk now on his lips. A pit of unease settles in my stomach, his smirk reminding me too much of Alexander's. But that's where the physical similarities end.

"Some call me the first one, some the White Spirit, others the true Alpha King. But you, little Crystalline, would have called me Father if times had been different." Shocked, I back away, unable to comprehend what this man just said. Father... as in my biological father. But that's not true. How could a man who claims to be the true Alpha King be my father when he clearly isn't from the twenty-first century?

"I know this is hard to hear-"

"You think?" I scoff, cutting this man off while I try to comprehend his statement.

"-But the truth is I am your biological father, and you Crystalline are the Lost Princess." I trip over a rock in my haste to back away, the shock of his statement causing me to lose focus on my surroundings. I brace for the impact of my body hitting the dirt, but instead I fid myself cradled in a warm embrace. The scent of moonflowers once again reaches me, mixed with the scent of the river I always found myself sitting by. It calms me, relaxing my mind from the chaotic state this wolf's words created.

"Careful, hun. This may be the dreamscape but you can still injure yourself." His voice is soft, carrying a tone that I have only heard other pups receive, the tone of a loving father.

"How... I was raised by Queen Clarice and King Alexander. How can I be the lost Princess?" I ask, tears filling my eyes and falling down my cheek as I question the man with disbelief.

"You know the legend of how I became a wolf, right?" He asks, and I nod.

"You were the leader of a wolf pack, a regular wolf pack, before cities and towns were made. You roamed the forest with your pack, coming and going from small tribes like a spirit on the wind until one day you laid your eyes on a young girl who caught your attention. For years, you would be her shadow, protecting her from kidnappings, vicious animals and other dangers." I begin, looking towards the forest and seeing the faint image of a building... of the Palace I grew up in. But it seems different. Gone are the ivy that climbs the wall facing the north, the electric lighting that had been placed in at the turn of the century to modernize the place, the crumbling tower that used to house a powerful witch is now brand new, as if untouched by the elements.

"Then one day, creatures enslaved by the sun that we now know as vampires conspired with rogue wolves to kill the humans that continued to grow in number and take over the territory. Your pack, catching wind of this, rushed to the village where the now young maiden lived only to be too late.

Rogues and vampires had slaughtered and bled dry everyone there or taken and Turned those they wanted as mates into vampires themselves. You let out a lone, heartbreaking howl, your heart broken from losing the one you wanted as a mate. The maiden watched from the dreamscape with the other Gods and Goddesses, tears streaming down her face when Goddess Morai gave the maiden two options. Become a Goddess herself and live with the wolf that loves her or continue down the path of death to be reincarnated." I continue, catching a smile on Spirit's face as he too joins me in looking over at the Palace.

"Luna became the first Moon Goddess, making an agreement to take the mantle five hundred years after learning to use her powers. During my howl, I felt my body shift and soon found myself laying on the cold hard floor as a human. Could you imagine my surprise when my pack also shifted, their mates also werewolves." He chuckles, a smile playing on my lips. I can picture the confusion now, the first werewolves feeling the pain of the shift but in reverse, how their wolf body would have formed and changed into a human one. The scene of them trying to walk on two legs must have been comical as well.

"I can imagine a few questioning how it happened and wonder who caused this magic." I answer, nudging his shoulder with mine playfully. Something in me seems to accept this wolf as he has not shown any hostility towards me. Even if I am still trying to figure out his motives.

"I still felt my broken heart while my pack and their mates felt a stronger love with each other, a tingle and electrifying shock we call the mate bond. And then I smelled it, her scent of moonflowers. The full moon shone down on where I stood and as if made of moon dust, and your mother appeared. As you know, we married and built our kingdom, then had your brother and your twin sister." A stabbing pain in my heart at the mention of the mate bond has me bending forward, gasping for breath and tears in my eyes. I thought this man mentioned it being the dreamscape, how could I feel the pain of rejection so strongly here?

"It's okay, just breath through the pain." With the scent of the river and moonflowers and the feel of gentle arms wrapping around me, I lean into my father's embrace, the feeling of love easing the feeling of rejection.

"This pain, it is real and no matter where your soul is, you will feel it. There is a reason behind it but unfortunately, I am sworn to secrecy from Goddess Morai." I nod at his answer, confused by his words but accepting that if the Goddess of Destiny has her hand in this, I just have to accept it and move on.

"Why did I not grow up with you, mother and my siblings?" I ask, clinging to my father and letting the pain ebb away. Someone made me miss the chance of growing up with love.

"Your brother. His name has changed over the centuries from Drathnid, to the current name Lupus. But thankfully the community of your current era knows him as his true name, Prince Coro. I knew he was jealous when you and your twin Selene were born. He bonded with Selene, always wanting to be a big brother to her. It kept us from being suspicious of him even if Witch Cassandra and the Maids told us other wise. In the shadows, he kept tormenting you, until one day you went missing." My father answers, a deep sigh ending his words as he caresses my face, his sad eyes looking over my features.

"No one suspected him as he was taking care of Selene. For years we searched, until we gave up hope. Luna had to train Selene as the next Moon Goddess and I had to train Coro as the next King. But something kept me from giving him the crown even after he found his mate and had pups of his own." Hearing the names of my brother, I frown thinking of history class and the war caused by Alpha Drathnid. If I am correct, he is the one that nearly killed off all witches. Lupus is a recent name, one that has been reported as the Rogue King by the council. A man that has kidnaped, tortured and raped many wolves for many years. But Prince Coro is one I learned about with my tutor. He is the ancestor of Alexander, the one I thought was my ancestor as well. It turns out I was wrong.

"The day I decided to give him the crown was the day before your mother was to ascend as the Moon Goddess. Luckily, or unluckily depending on the perspective, Goddess Morai came barging through the doors, anger radiating off of her small frame, with Witch Cassandra and many other trailing behind. There were stacks of books and the truth of your kidnapping mixed with the deeds Coro committed was revealed. A fight ensued and he escaped, killing his mate and the unborn pup as a way to prevent us from using them as leverage to capture him. Thankfully, his ten-year-old daughter was saved by Cassandra casting a protection barrier around her, and we were able to keep her safe. She created the current line of royals that now rule." A tear slips down his face, the memories of losing me and the betrayal of his son must be too hard to deal with. I stay silent, allowing my father time to sort out his emotions that still seem to have a strong hold over him even after all these centuries later. I cannot even begin to imagine how he feels.

"What did Coro have planed for me?" I ask after some time has passed and I feel that my father has stabilized. Although I am unsure if I want to know the answer, I have to know in order to live as a Rogue for the time being.

"He made a pact with a Witch, a very dark Witch. You were supposed to be kidnapped then killed so that he would have no contest for the throne. But Morai intervened, and the carriage the Witch and you were in was hit with an accident. Moonflowers swallowed you, keeping you in a stasis, if you would. It wasn't until eighteen years ago did the moonflowers let you free." A soft breeze blows past us, the scenery shifting as if someone pressed fast-forward on a screen. I watched as a small town was formed, as houses, shops and farms were created. I watch the Palace age over time, the white brick slowly becoming discoloured with the elements.

One thing that never changed is the moonflower meadow that we sat in. Then things stopped, and my father and I remained the only ones on the hill looking at the familiar pack lands that I grew up with. I watch a familiar face walking along the river in a flowing gown, her tear-stained face one I both wished to see and never see again. The late Queen Clarice, the woman that raised me, sat in the middle of the moonflower meadow. I take a step forward, wanting to rush to her, but a hand stops me.

"We can't interact with her. This is the memory of the moonflowers; I'm sorry." Father whispers, and I nod, tears threatening to spill once more. We watched in silence until the sounds of crying could be heard and the late Queen jumps, turning towards the sound until the scene changes and she and the crying are gone.

"When the late Alpha Queen mated the current Alpha King, it turned out she was barren. She kept it to herself, knowing that Alexander would kill her in order to find a mate that will give him an heir. One day, she stumbled upon the moonflower meadow, one neither your mother nor I had found, and found you still a newborn. It was perfect timing because Alexander was going to war with the vampires and would be gone for years. She told him the day he left that she was pregnant, and knowing you were safe, she left you in the safety of the moonflowers. For the next few months, she was attended to by her maids, the very same ones who raised you and were sworn to secrecy of your origin. You still were kept as a newborn and only cried twice. The first time was when she stumbled upon the meadow, and the second time when she picked you up and took you home. No one noticed the moonstone had fallen or was left in the moonflower meadow until you found it and put it on. That must have been a shock to Clarice." I smile, thinking back to the day she watched me find the necklace I treasure, her begging me to not go near the flowers with fear, but something called to me in the sea of white and green. I always wondered why she was so terrified of me entering the moonflower meadow but knowing now that she found me there made sense. She probably thought I would disappear just as fast as I had appeared to her.

"She was so mad at me. But at the same time, I think she had a feeling of who I truly am." I agree, turning away from the scenery behind me and looking to my father. Everything he has shown me proves I am his daughter and my instinct tells me to trust him. So with hope that this man will not abuse me the way Alexander had, I place my trust in him.

"So what do I do now?" I ask. A flame is ignited in me and revenge is what I wanted. I want revenge towards my brother, who took me away from our family. I want revenge for my mother, for Queen Clarice, against Alexander for how he treated Clarice and me. And finally, I want revenge against Narin for rejecting me and choosing Alexander.

"You train, build a pack of your own and take back the Royal Pack as the true heir. I will ask Luna and Selene to contact Geminie as she can stay in the dreamscape longer, but our time is up. Become strong, my daughter..."

Chapter 8 – Allies

"We need to start her training as soon as possible. With Prince Coro's antics becoming even more dangerous than the next, who knows what can happen in the next few years." A voice with a musical lilt floats through the air, reaching my ears as consciousness slowly returns.

"Trust me, Crysta can take anyone down." Matrix retorts with a huff to this mysterious person.

"I believe she can, but her brother is a trickier person. He has ways of killing without a trace." Another voice, one I recognize as Geminie, argues back.

"A year after we learned that Lupus was actually Coro, many smaller packs were taken over by Soulless. Not one person from the three packs he attacked survived." A deeper voice chimes in. I frown, deciding that now is a good time to wake up if the wolves in the room decided to continue talking about me and my brother. I need to know what they know in order to prepare myself for whatever fate has in store for me.

With a sigh, I open my eyes and am met with a ceiling of red fabric above me, realizing I am laying on a canopy bed. The room smells like lavender and mint, the bedding holding the same scent. It both calmed and invigorated me, clearing the fog of leaving the dreamscape from my mind. Turning to the sounds of the voice, I notice Geminie with her mate sitting close together on a loveseat, her pup playing on the floor with Amberle's pups. On a separate couch, Dominic sits watching Amberle pace the floor, his mate's movements full of agitation and anger.

"Fire, come sit. You can't let what happened get to you." The Alpha of Blood Moon sighs out, holding a hand out to his fiery mate. Watching her pause her steps, Amberle runs a finger through her locks before joining her mate on the couch and curling into his side.

"I'm sorry, Ice. I just can't understand how a father can treat his pup like the way Alexander treated Crystalline." At her statement, I feel a pang in my chest and clutch my fingers around the necklace, taking a moment to calm myself before making my presence known. My eyes sting with unshed tears as I think back to what Spirit, my real father, told me.

"It's because Alexander isn't my father." I state, the room growing silent as I push myself off of the bed and into a sitting position. Six pairs of eyes stare back at me. A woman with long black hair and pale skin sitting in an armchair watching me curiously captures my attention first.

"But I have a feeling you all knew this." I state, the women before me each giving a slight nod.

"All but me, apparently! For Goddess' sake, your mother said she was pregnant with you!" Matrix cuts in, practically throwing himself from the chair and running to my side, wrapping me safely in a hug. I take in his comforting scent, allowing a few tears to fall as my arms wrap around him. He had defended me, prepared for our escape and stayed loyal to me. If only he had been my soulmate and not Narin.

"I am so glad you are okay, Crystalline; you've been asleep for eight days." He whispers, relief flowing through our bond. Hugging him back, I take a moment to collect my thoughts and just enjoy the embrace of my best friend and accept the fact I was asleep for eight days since the ball, since the rejection. I am happy that Matrix is here, keeping his promise to always be by my side, through thick and thin. He may not be my mate, but he is definitely someone I can rely on right now, someone I can trust wholeheartedly while we figure out the mess I got myself in.

"King Spirit, my real father and the first Alpha King, called my soul to him." I answer, feeling Matrix gently wipe the tears from my cheeks.

"I had a feeling a Royal called you." Geminie sighs, giving me a sympathetic look.

"How was your first trip to the dreamscape?"

"Enlightening. My father said he would have my mother Luna and your mother contact you for my training." I answer, slightly confused.

"It has something to do with you being able to stay in the dreamscape longer than me." I continue. Geminie groans, running a hand through her hair as she leans back against the love seat, turning to look at her mate who smiles at her amused.

"Sorry, love, but Goddess work will be taking my time away from you." She tells him with a sigh, Ariven chuckling.

"I had a feeling that may happen. Alex already said he will handle the pack while we are away. Just make sure you and our unborn pup stay safe." He reassure her, placing a soft kiss on Geminie's forehead.

"You are the best, and so is Alex. We should definitely give him, Missy and Lizaria a vacation after this." A pang of jealousy at their affection forces me to look away. They look so happy and in love and I wished I had that with my mate. Instead I am left to deal with this pain of rejection and being turned Rogue.

"The Queen lied, didn't she." A statement, not a question, pulls the conversation back on track and away from what Geminie and Ariven were discussing. Pulling away from Matrix, I look towards the owner of the voice and notice the black haired, pale skin woman staring at me with deep indigo eyes.

"Yes. Alexander is sterile and can't have pups. I always thought it weird that the pack whores he kept never gave him another pup, and now I know why." I stand from the bed and make my way towards this mysterious woman. Holding my hand out to her, she stands and takes it in her own, shaking it firmly.

"Crystalline, but you already know this." I chuckle.

"Ira, Priestess of the Temple of the Moon Goddess." Ira greets me, a smile on her face. I nod, happy to know that we were in a neutral area. The Temple of the Goddess is the safest place for me right now with news of me being rejected and disowned as the heir to the werewolf throne.

"So your mother lied about being pregnant with you?" Ariven asks, directing the conversation back to the previous topic.

"No, my mother was pregnant with me." I answer, confused. I just explained that I was King Spirit and Queen Luna's daughter.

"What Ariven means is did Queen Clarice lie about being pregnant?" Ira explains, chuckling at my confusion. My eyes widen with realization and I quickly apologize for the misunderstanding. I had accepted the fact that Queen Luna is my birth mother, but my heart will always consider Queen Clarice as my mother as well.

"Yes, my adopted mother, Clarice, lied about being pregnant. She was also infertile and could not have pups. When Alexander went to war eighteen years ago just after his mate found me hidden in a moonflower meadow, she faked her pregnancy. On the day she supposedly gave birth, she came and gathered me from the meadow." I answer, running a hand through my messy hair and realizing someone had take it down some time between passing out at the ball and before I woke up.

"How is that even possible?! My mother was a lady-in-waiting for your mother!" I turn to see the disbelief on Matrix's face, his head held in his hands as he realizes his mother kept a secret from him for eighteen years.

"She was sworn by a royal order to keep my real birth a secret. Your mother and the other ladies-in-waiting could not tell a soul or they would be killed." I answer Matrix, sending him a sympathetic smile.

"So how did Clarice find you, Crystalline? Everyone has been searching for you for centuries." Ira asks, her musical voice catching my attention. I frown, trying to remember the conversation with my father, my mouth opening and closing as I try to word the answer that I am still trying to wrap my own mind around.

"Long story short, Coro had a Dark Witch kidnap me in hopes of killing me and removing me from the throne. But Morai intervened, and I was saved by the Goddess of Destiny." I begin, closing my eyes and letting out a long sigh.

"Unfortunately, I fell into the moonflower meadow, and with magic being abundant then, the flowers hid me and put me into a stasis where I never aged, stuck as a newborn until the time was right." Being the only explanation I can give everyone, I feel Matrix shift from the bed until he is behind me, placing something over my shoulders that I soon realize is my bear skin blanket before pulling me into his arms once more.

I let the information settle as silence takes over everyone and I lean into the comforting embrace of my friend. We grew up together, our mothers were best friends. It doesn't surprise me that his mother Lianna was sworn to secrecy when it came to the safety of the heir to the throne.

"Well, now that we know what happened to our Lost Princess here, I think it's time we start preparing." Ira breaks the silence that settled in the room. Turning to look at the wolves gathered, I catch a knowing look passing between Amberle and Geminie, concerned for what this means.

"What are we preparing for?" I ask the Priestess warily, my hands clenching Matrix's shirt. I just want a few days to settle my broken heart and mind, and some time to write out the information my father gave me when he summoned me to the dreamscape. I don't think I can handle anything more thrown my way.

"For war, Princess. You will need to take back your throne and kill Coro. And for that, you need allies." Ira answers, her indigo eyes staring right into my own.

"I think Crystalline can use a few days to settle in first. She has already been through a lot." Dominic chimes in, winking a blue eye at me and taking Ira's attention away from me. I mouth a silent thank you, pressing closer to Matrix.

"She also needs to train." Ira sighs.

"Ira, Crystalline must be in shock." Geminie chimes in gently, climbing to her feet and taking the Priestess' hand in hers.

"Do you remember when I learned I was the daughter to the Moon Goddess, how I needed to take in the information before meeting my mother and father?" She continues, Ira letting out a sigh of defeat.

"I guess you are right, Little Wolf. Fine, Crystalline, take a week to get yourself settled. But do know that a war is brewing because of your brother. The sooner you train, the sooner we can get you ready to defeat him." With that, Ira leaves the room and a weight feels lifted off my shoulders.

"I know you slept for eight days, but the rest of us barely have. We were all communicating with our allies explaining the details of your rejection and return. Lets just say Alexander has lost a large amount of support." Geminie states once Ira is out of the room. Now that she is closer to me, I can see the dark bags under her eyes, and I frown.

"I do need some alone time, if that's okay. Why don't all of you go get some rest, then?" I suggest, taking my cousin, no, niece's hand and smiling gently at her.

"I am not leaving you, Crysta." Matrix protests, his arms tightening around me.

"Fine. Alone time plus Matrix." I sigh, getting a chuckle from Geminie and a smirk from everyone else. Geminie says her goodbye, squeezing my hand as Ariven gathers their daughter in his arms. Amberle comes towards me, leaning forward to nuzzle her cheek against mine and promising that everything will be fine in the end before she leaves with her own family. Dominic carries their son and the twins wave happily at me. Now it is just Matrix and I left standing alone.

"You need sleep, Trix." I whisper softly, breaking the silence between us. His face has a shadow of stubble along his cheeks, and the bags under his eyes are so dark that I worry he may lose his sanity and turn Soulless.

"Only if I can hold you in my arms." He states his voice deep and holding emotion that I do not want to decipher right now. There is already too much going through my mind to deal with Matrix and I's relationship. I sigh helplessly, agreeing to letting him hold me and quickly find myself being carried to the canopy bed with Matrix covering us in my bear skin blanket. Before I can even yell at him he is already fast asleep.

"You're an idiot." I mumble, my fingers moving through his messy hair.

Chapter 9 – A Breath of Freedom

Sitting outside with fresh air surrounding me, I sit down on the grass, leaning my back against a sturdy oak tree while facing the temple. A day has passed since waking up, and as promised, Ira gave me my space. She also gifted me a set of leather-bound journals and a few high quality pens, telling me that I look like the type of wolf who needs to write out her emotions. I thought the Priestess would be hard to get along with, but she has surprised me with how motherly and caring she is.

Around me are trees of various shapes, the forest spreading out behind me with a clearing full of wildflowers and moonflowers in front of me. I smile and draw the scene before me, the floral scent comforting after years of walking through the moonflowers back in the Royal Pack.

"I see you found this spot." I jump, looking to my right to see Ariven leaning against a tree, his forest green eyes holding amusement at my reaction.

"Yes, I find it to be relaxing here." I answer warily. For a man over six feet tall, Ariven moves as silently as a Tracker.

"It is. Geminie and I first met here. She actually shifted for the first time right in this very field." He points to a spot where the wildflowers are blooming and I smile. To think, this burly looking wolf met my niece in a place like this.

"Was it love at first sight?" I ask, wanting to know more about Geminie's past.

"I am not sure. I will say it was a shock to learn later on that she would be my new Alpha. I still have the first picture of her saved to my phone, want to see it?" Ariven answers, peaking my interest at the mention of a photo of Geminie when she was my age. Climbing to my feet, I slowly walk towards Ariven who has taken out his phone, the latest Samsung smartphone, and watch as he scrolls through his photos.

He finally finds what he is looking for and turns his screen towards me. I frown, realizing he has to bend down slightly to allow me to see the screen as the top of my hair barely reaches his chest. Taking his hand, I move it so that the screen is visible without the glare of the sun and let out a gasp of surprise.

A live photo, one that looks like a regular picture until you click on it, is seen on the screen. A pure white wolf stands in the middle of the field. Her silver-grey eyes hold a look of confidence and triumph in their depth. Her white fur is full and healthy, the gentle breeze flowing through it, causing the sun to reflect off of it like a prism. Hues of different pastel colours constantly changing direction in the live photo where each ray of sun hits, the wild flowers dancing around her. A tuft of long fur, almost like bangs, covers the left side of her face. The final touches are the small patches of silver fur with swirls and stars climbing up part of her paws. Her wolf form is so much younger than what I have seen in our alliance howl a week ago and it is clear that her fur has matured over the years.

"This was taken five years ago. I still remember her growling at me for surprising her." Ariven chuckles. I can feel the love for his mate radiating off of him and hold in the whimper from the pain the mate bond I have with Narin causes. I want the love that Geminie and Ariven have.

"It wasn't until her powers started developing that her silver-grey eyes started to turn into the moon-white they are now. She can still see like anyone else, it's just the Power of the Goddess blood running through her." Ariven explains before I can ask the question, distracting me from the broken mate bond. I smile, looking at the picture once more and wonder if Selene looked like this.

"Could you take a picture of me and Gem in wolf form here later?" I ask sheepishly, watching as the Alpha wolf before me puts his phone away.

"Of course. Maybe some time this week, we can all relax and have a picnic here, and Gem can explain more about the dreamscape to you." He agrees. My face breaks into a grin, excited to have an opportunity to learn more about the dreamscape and how I can enter it.

"Anyways, how are you holding up? I know you've been through a lot." Ariven asks, taking a seat on the grass and patting the spot beside him for me to join. I sigh while sitting beside him, clutching the journal in my hands while looking at the wildflowers before me.

"I don't know how to feel to be honest. Confused, scared, upset and betrayed are just the surface." I start, a sad smile replacing my grin.

"I used to think that Coro was my ancestor, the reason why I am here. Technically, he is still the reason why I am here but also the reason why I never grew up with my real parents, why I never got to experience life with my twin." I continue. I jump when tears I had no idea had fallen from my eyes, Ariven giving me a sympathetic smile.

"It must be hard. I think you should talk with Geminie." He suggests, ruffling my hair playfully.

"Why?" I ask, swatting his hand away and sticking my tongue out at him as he laughs at me.

"She went through something similar. She was kidnapped at birth by the parents of Alex, our Beta and her older brother. She grew up hated and abused because of Bastian and Jasmine Blake. If anyone understands the struggle you are going through, it's her." He answers. I look away from him and down at my journal, biting my bottom lip as I think over what I just learned about Geminie. To think, someone so powerful went through something so horrible.

"And if you want to learn about toxic sibling behaviour, talk to Amberle. I think her sister Mia is still out there somewhere slandering Amberle as we speak." Looking up, I see Geminie walking towards us, her prismatic hair tied into a bun with Destiny running around the flowers. I smile at the she-wolf as she sits beside me, wrapping me in a hug.

"So, I was thinking that instead of an aunt-and-niece relationship, you can think of me as a big sister and Ariven as your big brother. We are family after all." Leaning into her warmth, I close my eyes and take in her calm energy, feeling myself calm down. I can sense her sincerity and the idea of having a loving family with these two wolves makes the coldness the rejection in me seem less isolating.

"I'd like that." With a small whisper I agree, pulling away to look at Geminie who smiles down at me with love in her eyes.

"Good. If you need anything, I am just a call away. Okay?"

"Okay." Looking over at Ariven, I see a flash just in time to realize he had taken a picture of Geminie and I, a grin splitting his face. Maybe with their help, I can find my own strength and become an Alpha as strong as these two. Between Ira's training and the love from my small family, I know that I can make it through these next few weeks while learning to deal with my heartbreak and discovering just who I truly am.

Chapter 10 – Lessons

Groaning, I shut the history book on the desk in frustration, wondering whose god-awful idea it was to have me learn the history of wolves—the entire history of wolves, might I add. Deep inside the library in the Temple of the Goddess surrounded by shelves full of books, Ira watches over me, her sharp, knowing gaze showing her amusement at my frustration.

"You need to know everything, Crystalline. A knowing ruler is the best ruler." She states, turning back to the paperwork spread out on her own desk. I sigh, watching the she-wolf for a moment, wondering how she kept her black hair so pristine in a bun on top of her head, how her simple outfit of a green dress and black heels can look so elegant and regal on her. I hope that I can look as queenlike as she does.

"I get that. It's just, considering I grew up in the palace, I am quite sure I know all that needs to be known." Laying my head on the desk, I close my eyes for a moment to take a break. The smell of the old books and stone shelves bring a sort of peace to me even if I find reading constantly to be torturing to my mind.

"Do you know how Coro managed to live for all these years? Or how he amassed his powers?" Ira asks, her voice light yet holding a tone of inquiry. Taking a moment to think, I realize that the Priestess has me. She knows I do not know this answer but still asked.

"No. Would the answers be in these books?" Opening my eyes, I see her smiling as she stands, motioning me to follow her. With a sigh, I sit up, push my chair back and stand. It has been two weeks since I first came to the Temple. The first week, I spent sorting out my mind. With Geminie and Amberle's help, I was soon able to find information about my disappearance in the library. Then on the eighth day, Ira came and took me back here, a stack of books already waiting to be read. Now, with a week of being in this library and getting to know the Priestess and learning that she has been the Priestess for three hundred years since taking over after her mentor's death,

I have learned she would rather show and not tell me any of the answers, preferring that I discover them myself.

Leading me down rows of shelves to the far right side of the library, I notice the books slowly becoming older and older the further we go. The air becomes dusty, the smell of slightly decaying paper and preservatives to keep the words written it as pristine as possible causing me to sneeze. I watch as dusty shelves appear every so often, mixed in with the older books, until I notice the books turning from leather-bound journals to baskets full of scrolls. One catches my eye, a basket labeled "The Tale of the Lost Princess." This is one that I had not found when Amberle, Geminie and I explored the library, so I reach out to take it, wanting to know what was said about me when I went missing.

"Leave it, you can look at it on our way out." Jumping, I turn to see Ira staring at me with a smirk. Of course, I listen to the wolf, knowing she is doing everything in my best interest. Pulling my hand away, I take one last look at the scroll before continuing with Ira and watch as the shelves slowly become emptier with less books and scrolls as we pass. Something about the air changes, as if charged by magic and electricity. Surprisingly, I feel calm, almost as if returning home. Curious to know the reason behind the air becoming denser and denser with each step, I continue behind Ira, my eyes scanning the shelves that grow sparser until finally we reach our destination and stand in front of a set of wooden doors.

"This door is the entrance to the restricted area." Ira begins, running her hand over the intricate pattern of leaves and vines intertwining with the phases of the moon.

"Only the Priestess of this temple, Witch Cassandra, and a wolf with royal blood can enter." She continues, stepping back and motioning me to open the door. Tentatively, I place my hands against the handles, magic flowing through me the moment my skin contacted the metal. With out warning, the doors fly open forcing me to release the handles and jump back in surprise. Just how powerful is the witch who created the magic seal to this room.

"Inside is information that only a few have privilege to look through. You'll understand why. Just know you only get an hour a day inside the room. If you don't leave within the hour, you'll be trapped here until someone can open it from the outside." With that warning, Ira turns and walks away, leaving me alone to face to restricted area. Deciding that this is an opportunity I cannot let go, I take a deep breath and walk inside. The first thing I feel when entering the room is the pulsating magic that surrounds me, magic I did not think could be this strong. The second is the feeling of being watched.

"Hello?" I call out, my voice echoing around the stone walls of the small room. The silence that follows is eerie, causing goosebumps to form on my skin and my once confident footsteps to slow with caution. No shelves line the walls and no books are in sight. The only thing I can see is a softly glowing moonstone that sits in the middle of the room reminding me of the full moon on a cloudless night. Curious, I continue walking towards the large moonstone, realizing that the sphere is larger than a bowling ball and smile. Something inside me tells me this crystal has all the answer I need, but how to I get them.

Apprehensively, I reach out towards the stone and think about one question—How did Coro become immortal? As soon as my fingertips connect with the smooth, warm moonstone, the world fades away.

◆◆◆

Opening my eyes, I find myself standing in the middle of a forest. The area seems familiar, like I know this place but can't seem to figure out how.

"You said you would help me!" A deep voice roars, forcing me to turn to find the one screaming.

"I did, my Prince, but someone intervened." A female voice answers meekly, her soft voice quivering.

"Well, now they know I tried to kill that wench. I thought you said everything would be fine!" Walking quietly towards the voice, I peer out from behind an oak tree. Before me is a black-haired woman, her tanned skin and blue eyes gazing at a man before her. Something about this man seems familiar. His black hair, fair skin, and blue eyes are ones I know well. I have seen paintings of this man before, of the man who I thought was my ancestor. Before me stands my brother, Prince Coro.

"I thought everything was fine. When the carriage tipped over, the Princess vanished. I though she had died as well." The witch argues. My eyes widen and I realize that the two are talking about the night I was supposed to be killed, the night Morai saved me.

"Well, now they are out to kill me, thanks to your blunder. You owe me for what I paid you."

"And what is it that you want, Prince Coro?" The witch asks. I can taste the fear in the air as she watches Coro and I frown. Whatever Coro wants will not be good.

"Immortality. I want immortality, Avilla." I gasp, wanting to rush forward to stop this witch from doing anything, but I trip.

•••

As my body falls to the ground, my vision once again fades to black. In minutes I find myself back in the restricted area, my body feeling weak as I think about what I just witnessed. Coro gained his immortality through a witch. I will need to look through the library for anything involving Witch Avilla and see what spells she specialized in. With Coro living as long as he has, I need to know what spell was used and whether or not I can truly defeat my brother.

With a sigh, I turn to leave, deciding that knowing when Coro first gained his immortality is a great start and that if I need answers for anything else relating to bringing him down, I can come here. For now, I need to learn more from Ira about what I missed the last few centuries and make a list of what I genuinely want to know after speaking to her. She seems to know more than what she lets on, so let's see if she knows about Avilla. With a smile, I look back at the moonstone, feeling a warm glow from it, before walking out and hearing the doors closed behind me.

I have other lessons I need to learn today, one being a good fight with Ariven in a few hours. So right now, I plan to read some of the older scrolls in the area outside the restricted area and start learning from the beginning of the werewolf creation.

•••

I groan, landing hard on my back for the umpteenth time on the hard ground, wincing when I try to move. Ariven and I have been sparring for the last hour, the former Temple resident using every trick he has learned against me and making me realize just how weak the training at the Royal Pack is.

One thing is for sure, I will have to re-establish a better training routine when I claim the throne.

"I think you might have broken something." His deep voice calls out as Ariven walks over to where I lay, helping me gently to stand.

"No, I think I just fractured a rib." I wince, leaning against him for support. It felt nice having someone support me after a fair spar, someone like Ariven who, since the time I woke up finding out my true identity, has treated me like a little sister. Geminie never once showed the jealousy that other she-wolves would show, instead praising him for being a good big brother to me, making me smile and laugh along with her. It felt nice having a loving family.

"So, I heard you went to the restricted area today." He states, helping me walk, well limp, to a bench and I nod, wincing slightly when I move too fast and jostle the fractured rib.

"Ira took me there to learn about Coro." I answer before wincing.

"Learn anything useful?" I can tell he is trying to keep my mind off the pain as my healing takes time to kick in, and I am grateful for it.

"I learned one thing about him that I need to research first. But I felt a little tired after the vision the room showed me. I feel like I need to be careful before using that room again and really think about what I need to know before going." I say through gritted teeth, cursing as I am helped to sit down, wrapping my arm around my right side and holding onto the area where pain radiates.

"That's a good idea. Whenever Gem goes into that room, she comes out pale and exhausted with a haunted look in her eyes. Sometimes I worry she won't ever come out again." Sitting down beside me, I watch as Ariven looks down at his clasped hands, a worried look etched on his face.

"I guess you've never been inside?" I ask, turning to look outside the window and stare at the forest.

"No, and I fear the day Destiny and her unborn sibling has to enter that room." He states, his words filled with the care and love for his daughter causing my heart to ache and leaving me feeling jealous.

A silence settles beside us, leaving the two of us to our thoughts while my healing kicks in on my fractured rib. Hearing from an outsider's perspective about the restricted area confirms that I made the right decision to wait until

I am truly ready to use the moonstone again. I don't want to admit it, but the vision took more out of me than I expected, and because of this, it made training a lot harder today.

For now, I just need to focus on becoming stronger and smarter if I want to claim what is rightfully mine.

Chapter 11 – Bittersweet Decision

I sit in front of the moonstone orb, questioning whether I should put my hands on it. Three weeks have passed since Ira brought me to this room, and each day I would spend an hour either before training or after training, staring at it, wondering if I am ready to know the answers to my other questions. Sadly, the answer has been no. I am not ready because there is so much I need to learn, so much I need to do before I can ask the questions needed for me to beat Coro and Alexander. I have barely learned about Avilla the Dark Witch of the North. Little is known about her, and so before I can learn how Coro gained his immortality, I need to learn about Avilla.

"You ready to go?" I jump as Geminie comes up behind me, with Destiny in her arms.

"Almost. I just wanted to spend an hour alone and figured this would be the safest place." I admit, standing and making my way towards the Future Goddess. I smile at Destiny, taking the toddler into my arms when she reaches out to me and resting her against my hip, placing a kiss on the two year old's forehead.

"Well you'll be leaving in a few hours. I think this trip will be good for you since you've lived in the palace all your life." My friend states as the two of us walk out of the restricted area, the doors closing behind us. We navigate the labyrinth of shelves in the library, making our way out into the hall. I turn and look back at the room I have sat in for the last four weeks learning as much as I can and silently thank the ones who recorded the knowledge. It helped me make the decision to journey away from the werewolf world for a moment and learn more about life outside of the palace and werewolf community.

"You can always come visit and read more." Geminie states, a knowing look in her eyes as she takes Destiny from my arms and places the toddler on her feet, allowing her to run ahead of us.

"I know. I plan to at least every summer, maybe sooner if I can learn more about Avilla and what spells she created." I smile, following the Alpha wolf while we chase after her daughter and silently walk the temple halls towards the exit. I have to leave, to find my own answers first and grow stronger. Once we exit the temple and enter the parking lot, I look back at the building that has housed and protected me. This is the place where I learned the truth of myself and my family, and of what I need to do in order to grow stronger. I will have to move forward now, towards claiming the throne, but the road ahead will be difficult.

"Are you sure I can't come with you?" Turning towards the person that asked the question, I spy Matrix leaning against the Hummer gifted to me by Amberle. With a sad smile, I rush to my best friend and wrap my arms around him. He hugs me back, his face buried in my hair.

"You can't, Trix. I need to do this on my own." I answer, taking in his scent.

"But you need me. You need protection." He tries to argue and I sigh. As much as I love my best friend and his protective behaviour towards me, I can't grow into the Alpha Queen I want to be with him always keeping me safe.

"Matrix, I need you to train as well. Amberle and Geminie already said you can train in their packs while I do my own training and growing."

"Your pictures are spread all over the world already through the website. Alexander still believes you're biologically his and wants you captured alive to produce an heir." He continues, trying to argue his way into coming with me. With a sigh, I pull away from my friend and look him in the eyes, needing him to understand just how serious I am in doing this on my own.

"Matrix, they are after me, not you. If they see you with me, you'll be killed." I begin, holding up a finger to stop whatever protest he was ready to bring out.

"I will be staying in the human cities. If anyone tries to take me there, the laws of the humans will protect me. And if that doesn't work, I still have my silver dagger." I watch as he sighs in defeat, knowing that I am right and him coming with me will do more harm than good.

"Not only that, but Crystalline has a lawyer friend of mine to visit. He is an immensely powerful Vampire that has been around since her parents first came to rule and has her inheritance tucked away. She will be safe." Ira calls out behind me.

"On top of that, I hope this Vampire can help me find answers on Avilla and Coro. He is an Ancient and has a coven of his own. I am sure he can help me," I add with a smirk. Turning to face the Priestess, I make my way into her open arms, accepting the hug from her as well.

"Keep in touch, Princess." She whispers into my ear.

"I will. I promise." With this, she releases me and I say my goodbyes to the others, Ariven gifting me a set of silver throwing knives and Amberle expecting me to call every week. I realize I went from having only Matrix by my side to having a family of wolves who accept me for who I am, not just as the next ruler of the werewolves.

Sapphira and Esmerald hand me drawings they drew for me, their little faces looking sad that I have to leave. I spent days after training running around with these two on my back in the forest, being as playful as a pup, and have grown close to the twins.

"You two behave for your mommy, okay." I say to them, bringing them into a hug.

"We will, Aunty Crys." Sapphira answers. I ruffle her hair before turning and giving Brent and Destiny a hug as well. Hopefully soon, I can visit these pups and maybe have them join me in Toronto one summer.

With a sad smile, I climb into the driver's side of my new vehicle, a gift from Ira, and drive away, fighting back the tears of bittersweet happiness of leaving everyone behind, watching the trees that hide the Temple from view pass by me and the hidden gravel driveway becoming concrete roadway.

For the first time in my life, I feel like I am saying goodbye to my home and family.

Chapter 12 – A Journey with New Friends

I sigh as I pull over, my tears blurring my vision and making me unable to drive. It's been two hours since I left the temple and it takes everything not to turn back. But I can't. I have to keep going and make my way to Toronto so I can hide from Alexander and find my own way in life before I can take the throne. Taking deep breaths, I wipe away the tears and calm myself down, even with the feeling of homesickness kicking in harder than I expected.

Deciding I need some fresh air, I turn the Hummer off and step outside, making sure to bring my silver dagger with me before locking the vehicle. Thankfully, I had pulled into a rest stop that leads to a hiking trail, so no one would question a car left unattended here. With a grin, I walk into the forest, relishing in the freedom of being one with nature for a moment without any constraints.

The fresh air brings the scent of the forest to me and somewhere in the distance I can smell a river. I will miss this, miss the fresh air when I am in the city. I will have to make trips out of Toronto frequently to get this tranquil feeling that I have now. I find myself in a small clearing, my feet subconsciously leading me to the river I smelled.

The water rushes by and I think about Amberle and Geminie, how the girls would sneak me treats and wine even knowing I am still technically underage, how Dominic and Ariven would spar with me. I wonder if I will have a sparring partner in Toronto or if I will have to hunt down my brother's Soulless and fight them as training. I still wonder how the Soulless came to be and how they are connected to Coro. Maybe the answers I get about Avilla can give me this answer.

Then there is Matrix. We grew up together and wanted each other as mates. I don't know how I will be able to be without him on this journey but I will have to try.

An hour passes and my emotions settle. I know I can visit everyone, and I can't wait to be settled in the city and have them come visit. With a smile,

I start walking back to my car. It'll get late soon, and part of me doesn't want to camp in the woods.

Awwwwooooooooh

My foot steps pause at the sounds of a howl, one every wolf hates to hear. Soulless were near and that spells trouble. Rushing towards the direction the howl came from, I head deeper into the forest and off the hiking trail. The farther into the trees, the closer the stench of death and decay become. I realize that this stench is that of Soulless and inwardly curse. They are migrating closer to the Temple and I cannot allow any of them to attack the sacred place.

"Stay back, Alice!" A childish voice calls out, making me run faster. Children were in trouble, and a rush of fear that the Soulless is after them hits me. Scenting the air, I frown and realize two other wolves were near, meaning two children are facing off with the Soulless, and if I don't hurry soon, these two will become minced meat.

"Be careful, Blake!" a little girl cries out in warning. Thankfully, I am close by, and with a burst of energy, I find myself jumping off of a small cliff and landing in front of the two children, dagger at the ready as I take in the two Soulless baring their putrid fangs at two kids and now me.

"Who... Who are you?" The boy asks as soon as I straighten, deciding which Soulless to kill first.

"A friend. We can talk later." I reassure the two frightened kids. Without a second to spare, I race towards the Soulless on the left—an ex-Beta who had lost the majority of their weight—dodging a swipe of their claws and slashing at their paw with the dagger. I watch as it recoils in pain, the silver burning its flesh and giving me a moment to quickly slit their throat, inflicting a quick and painless death. Now, I cast my attention to the second Soulless.

This one eyes me carefully, as if its humanity is not too far gone. I have a feeling they are watching, waiting to see what the results would be. Something inside me tells me that I need to kill this wolf seeing as it holds the slight scent of a Tracker, and that instinct turns out to be correct. The wolf slowly backs away, watching me warily before turning tail and running off. Making sure the children are safe and that no predators are about, I rush after the Soulless, using the trees the way Amberle trained me to, and quickly catch up to the Soulless. Within moments, I had taken the lead and waited patiently before finally jumping off the branch and landing directly on its back. Although this won't kill the Soulless, it slows it down and gives me a chance to back away before they can sink their teeth into me.

"Coro sent you, didn't he?" I speculate, seeing a flash of recognition in the Soulless' eyes.

"Tell my brother I will find him and kill him, then." I chuckle, watching as the wolf's eyes glaze over in the way it does when a link is activated. Slowly stalking towards the wolf before me, I wait for its focus to return to me and when it does, I watch as fear clouds its face just as I sink my dagger into its neck, not bothering to dodge the attack and earning a wound on my arm. It's the price I have to pay to send the message to my brother. After making sure this Soulless has a painless and quick death, I rush back to where I left the children, shocked to see them still against the cliffs walls and waiting patiently for me.

"Thank you for saving us." The little girl smiles, the boy standing in front of her protectively.

"You're welcome. Why are you two out here alone?" I watch the two closely, deciding to lean against a tree a few feet away to give them their space while I clean and sheath my dagger now that there is no immediate threat.

"Why should we tell you?" The boy asks defiantly. Ah, the teenager attitude. Goodie.

"Because it's not normal for pups to be out alone without pack mates while carrying backpacks." I point out, nodding towards their packs on the floor just behind them.

"We ran away from our pack." The little one answers. Looking closely, I notice how gaunt their features are, realizing they were underweight.

"Alice, shut up!"

"No, Blake. She saved us, so she must be good!" I watch the two bicker and I sigh, pushing myself off from the tree and walking towards them, scooping their backpacks onto my shoulders.

"I am Crystalline Thorn. If you want, I am heading to Toronto and could use the company. I was even thinking about heading to McDonald's for some food." I smile at the two pups, seeing their eyes widen when they realize I am offering them a ride and some food.

"You won't take us back to our packs?" The boy asks.

"You ran away for a reason. So did I. Why don't you tell me all about it on the way to the city and we can stick together while we are at it?" I answer, jumping in surprise when someone takes my hand and notice the little girl beside me, a smile on her face.

"Can we go to one with a Play Place?" She sheepishly asks and I chuckle, bending down and lifting her into my arms, doing everything to keep the smile on my face when I realize just how light she is. I really need to get some food into her little body and get her and the boy healthy.

"We can definitely go to one with a playroom for you." With that, I carry her towards my Hummer, knowing the boy will follow me no matter what.

"I'm Alice Skylarke, and that's my older brother Blake." With a smile, Alice introduces herself and her brother Blake as well. I have a feeling these two have a story to tell, and when they are ready, I am all ears.

Chapter 13 – A Lawful Vampire

"Is this the place?" Blake asks as we pull into a parking lot. I smile at the pup turning to see his sister Alice fast asleep in the back seat, her golden hair shinning after our night in the motel room and having access to a proper bath.

"Yes. We can talk to the lawyer about making me your legal guardian." I answer, seeing the hope in the thirteen year old's eyes. With a chuckle, I climb out of the vehicle and make my way to Alice's side, opening the door and gently shaking her.

"Alice, we are here." I coo to the nine year old, watching her slowly open her eyes. She yawns as Blake joins us, still a little weary of me even after three days on the road getting to know one another. I know in time he will warm up to me, and I think that by taking care of his sister, he will see that I am no threat to them.

"Are we here?" The little pup mumbles as she wakes from her nap, rubbing her eyes. I chuckle, helping her unbuckle her seatbelt and lifting her into my arms. She is still so thin and I hope that with a few good meals, she will be able to grow to a healthy weight.

"Yes, we are here." I answer, tucking her hair out of the way before closing her door and locking the car. Making my way to the entrance of the building with the pups, I reach out and take Blake's hand to make sure the crowd of humans don't whisk him away from me, only releasing his hand once we make it safely in front of the doors. As soon as we enter the lobby to the fourteen-story office building, Blake shuffles closer to my side, his eyes wide yet cautious of all the humans mingling around us and going about their day.

[Relax, Blake. You are safe here.] I link the teen beside me, reaching out my hand for him to take. I am shocked yet extremely happy when his fingers interlock with mine, his trust in me protecting him and his sister making my heart melt. Hand in hand with Blake and Alice on my hip, we walk towards the reception desk where a woman sits. Scenting the air, I am surprised to see she is a witch, her hands moving on the keyboard before her while she converses with someone on the phone floating next to her ear. She holds up a finger to us, mouthing 'One Moment' to me and I nod, seeing how busy she is and decide to lead Blake to the sitting area just across from her desk.

"Can she be trusted?" Blake asks as we sit down, eyeing the witch. I chuckle, ruffling his blonde hair and settle into my chair, Alice already sleeping against my shoulder.

"Yes. Most witches can be trusted, especially ones that openly work with other supernaturals and around humans." I reassure, seeing him nod and his posture relaxing. This must be a shock to the young boy, traveling to a big city after running from his pack. Hopefully, he and Alice can open up about why they ran away while I talk with this lawyer and apply to be their guardian.

"Sorry for the wait, ma'am, I was dealing with an idiot Alpha." The witch apologizes, walking towards me with a smile and two large lollypops for the pups.

"It's fine. My name is Crystalline, and I am here to see Mr. Atticus." I stand, careful not to wake Alice as I release Blake's hand to shake her free hand.

"Oh, I am shocked you made it here so early! Atti has been waiting for you and told me to clear his schedule the moment you arrived. I just didn't expect you to bring pups." She exclaims happily, motioning for us to follow her as she takes us behind her desk to a door that leads directly to an elevator that we all file into. Blake takes my hand once again and shuffles closer, the witch pressing a button and shutting us in.

"I sent a link to Atti, this elevator will take us right into his office." She explains just as the floor begins to move and the feeling of us ascending higher makes my eyes widen in surprise. I have never been in an elevator before and judging by Blake's similar reaction, neither has he. The elevator ride is short-lived and the doors open to reveal a lavish office. A large wooden table with six chairs tucked around it greets us as we walk into the room.

"Crystalline, it is so good to finally meet you." A deep voice calls out, his accent a muted old English. Turning to face the source of the voice, I watch as a tall, tanned man walks towards me, his dark eyes holding fondness and something akin to pride and love. His scent is of mint and raspberry with a hint of iron, and I can't help but wonder if the iron comes from his need for blood in order to stay alive and not become feral.

"You look just like Luna did and the exact carbon copy of Selene. But that is to be expected as you are the twin to the second Moon Goddess and daughter of the first." He chuckles, giving me a hug on my right side, careful to not jostle the sleeping Alice before turning to look at the weary Blake hiding behind me.

"Are these your pups?"

"Uh no. I actually saved Blake and Alice from Soulless after leaving the Temple. Is it safe to assume you are Atticus?" I answer, asking my own question in the end as the witch bids us goodbye and leaves through the elevator. She must be busy, dealing with complaining customers and by the sounds of it, thick-headed Alphas. I do not envy the poor woman.

"Yes, I am. I have been your family's lawyer for centuries now, and I am excited to finally hand you your inheritance, young wolf." Atticus chuckles, motioning for me to take a seat at the table. Blake and I take the seat closest to us, the teen letting me place Alice on the couch first so that she can continue to sleep while Atticus walks towards his desk, rummages through a drawer and returns to the table with a file in hand.

"So first off, care to explain why you brought the pups?" Atticus begins.

"I am not a pup, I am thirteen!" Blake shouts, his eyes glaring at the vampire across from me. I sigh, placing a hand on the teen's shoulder and telling him to settle down before he wakes his sister, which seems to calm him some. He really is an overprotective brother.

"Okay, not a pup, then." The vampire concedes, sending me a wink and going along with Blake's outburst. I smile, sending him a silent thank you as Blake settles back into the seat, still glaring at the vampire who gives him a friendly smile, his fangs peeking out just below his top lip.

"As I mentioned, I saved them from Soulless and offered to bring them here with me. I want to be their guardian." I explain, running my hand through Blake's hair and watching the pup visibly relax with my touch. My heart breaks, seeing how a basic touch brought such comfort to him and wonder just what the siblings are hiding.

"I can help with that, but I need to know more to their story." Atticus agrees. I sigh, realizing that becoming their guardian might be a little difficult if Blake refuses to tell us why he and his sister were alone. But to my surprise, the teen looks at me, then at the couch where his sister slept, before looking at Atticus.

"If I tell you, will you promise not to send us back to our old pack?" He asks Atticus, his small features carrying a look of seriousness. I hold my breath, the sibling already knowing I would not send them back, but I can't say the same about this lawyer before us.

"Considering you are here with the Lost Princess; I can guarantee that I will never let you return to whatever pack you came from. I promise." Atticus's words seems to appease Blake as he takes a deep breath and looks out the window, staring out at Lake Ontario as he thinks over his words.

"Alice and I were orphaned when Alice turned three. Soulless snuck into the pack and killed our parents. I was seven at the time. We became Omega's instantly and because my sister is the only golden-haired wolf with blue eyes, she was put into a special class." I watch as his fists clench in anger at the mention of the class, wondering just what the two went through.

"If I wasn't at school, I was cleaning the pack house with other Omegas, barely able to see my sister. A week ago, I was lucky enough to work near the class Alice was in and that's when I learned what that class was about." Rage is simmering off of Blake by this point and something inside me tells me I am not going to like this answer. Without hesitation, I wrap my arms around him, running my fingers through his hair to help calm the furious pup, feeling angry myself at the pack they ran away from.

"What is that class about, Blake?" Atticus asks, reaching over to gently hold his clenched hand.

"They take orphaned girls with unique looks and train them to be bed warmers. When the girl turns twelve, they are used for sex by the top pack members." Blake whispers, a tear running down his face. I look to Atticus whose face is set in a grim look. Quickly, he stands and rushes to his desk, taking a laptop and bringing it to the table, promptly opening it.

"Blake, I need to ask. Is this pack called Nightmare Moon?" Atticus asks, turning the laptop to face Blake with the pack mentioned on display, the layout of every building easily recognizable. I shudder, realizing that Nightmare Moon is an ally pack of Alexander, and the unease I felt each time I had to visit the pack and meet the Alpha is finally explained.

"Yes. That's where the class is and where they keep the girls." Pointing to a building just on the edge of the territory. I frown, watching as Atticus turns the laptop around and type for a moment, Blake clinging to me and breathing in my scent. No wonder they are so malnourished and tired all the time, and why Blake has trouble trusting others.

"I just sent this information to Ira. We have had she-wolves escape from that pack and take refuge at the Temple. Geminie will take care of this issue, and I have a feeling Nightmare Moon will be no more now that we have two children who have escaped from there." Atticus explains as he closes the laptop, his flawless looking face holding a weariness I did not expect from someone who does not age.

"Blake, you are a very brave wolf for running away with your sister, and I promise that Crystalline will be your guardian now that we know you two are orphans and were abused. I have Heidi, the witch you met, getting the paperwork ready. I just need your last name."

"It's Skylarke. Blake and Alice Skylarke." Atticus nods, his eyes glazing over and I smile. Knowing that this vampire is helping these siblings stay together and letting me keep them by my side makes me happy.

"Okay. Heidi has the information and will bring the papers up after we deal with Crystalline." With that, Atticus opens the folder he brought to the table earlier, turning the contents to face me. Curious, I ask if it okay for me to look and once I see the vampire nod, I pull the folder towards me, taking a look at the first page and looking up in shock.

"Five billion?!" Blake winces as I shout in shock shushing me and reminding me his sister is sleeping. I apologize before looking down at the paper then back to Atticus who chuckles, getting up from his seat and moving to sit beside me, his manicured fingers taking the folder from my hand.

"You father left me with some decent gold to play with for your inheritance. I got bored at one point and invested into a few things for you when you decided to re-emerge. I have been the lawyer for the wolves born from Luna's and Spirit's bloodline for centuries and have helped them to invest in business and real estate for years." He explains, flipping the first page over to the next where the shock continues. I look at the ledger before me, noticing the list of assets.

"I own all of this?" I ask incredulous, catching Blake looking towards the papers as well and letting out a low whistle.

"Yes. This is a cosmetics business I opened up in your name. I mean, I used your money to create it but I own a few shares as well. This is a local gallery that was created a few hundred years ago and local artists sell their work. Of course, the gallery earns a commission to pay the five workers and utilities, but the rest of the money is profit for you." I listen as he goes down the list, explaining the businesses and the profit, how each one came to be or how it was bought, and how some properties are rented out. I thought I was penniless when I left the Palace. Instead, it turns out I am richer than the Royal Pack.

"I have a feeling you also have a hand in the profit as well." I chuckle, seeing a mischievous grin on the vampire's face.

"I mean, I hope you don't mind but I considered it payment for managing your assets. I still made you richer than the hundred gold left for you as the years passed by." He says flippantly, making me laugh.

"That's fine. I wonder why the Royal Pack is so poor if you could create amazing wealth like this." I ponder, flipping through the papers once more.

"I tired to get Alexander to listen to me, but that fool has no idea what is good for him." I chuckle at Atticus' grumbling, realizing that I may have made a great friend and ally.

"Atticus—" I start, getting cut off before I can continue.

"Please Crystalline, I have waited centuries for this. Can you call me Uncle Atti? Your father was my best friend and I watched Selene grow into a powerful Moon Goddess. Now I get to finally watch you become a fair and just Queen." His eyes holds familiar love at the mention of my family, the hope his words have that I will treat him the same way as my sister once did. Ira sending me here was a blessing in disguise, and when I get a cell phone and a home to settle into, I will have to call the Priestess to thank her.

"Uncle Atti, do you think you could help me keep investing and growing my funds? I also need a house while I live in Toronto for a few years." I continue, my eyes tearing up as he gentle pulls me into a hug and takes a deep breath of my scent.

"Of course, Crystalline. You can always call me for anything, and I will be there for you, Little One." He whispers. I came in needing a lawyer, and I will be leaving with an uncle, two pups of my own, and more money than I can fathom. I cannot be any luckier.

Chapter 14 – Temporary Home

I groan at the multiple boxes around the room, realizing that I should have paid for the moving crew to build the furniture for me. I am an idiot and thought it would be easy. Two weeks have passed since moving to Toronto and lucky for me, Uncle Atti let the pups and I live with him while I searched for a home of our own. Heidi helped me find a therapist—a witch name Hailey who is part of her coven—for Blake and Alice, the two needing help to process their experience within their old pack.

Five days ago after their first therapy session, Heidi called me to tell me about this large, six-bedroom, two-bathroom house with a finished basement. We were ecstatic and agreed to meet the realtor to see the house the next day. As soon as I saw the two-story building with a large backyard and a three-car garage, I knew instantly that it would be perfect. Without hesitation, I offered to buy the place outright with for two million dollars, an extra five-hundred thousand than the asking price.

"Crystalline!" A voice calls out as the front doors open.

"Upstairs, Uncle Atti." With a sigh, I lean against the wall and call as I call out to him, the vampire appearing within second.

"Hello, Little O– what's with all the boxes?" His greeting is cut off as he too scans the room with a multitude of boxes laying about.

"Furniture that needs to be built." My grumbled response brings an amused smile to his lips as he ruffles my hair.

"I told you to let the movers do it." He chuckles, pulling me to his side in a hug.

"I know. I should have listened but I wanted to try it on my own." I sigh. I had maids and Omegas help build the furniture. Not once have I done much by myself.

"Besides, the pups are with Heidi right now shopping for decorations for their rooms. I thought I would have time to build everything, but I clearly underestimated how much work it would be." With a groan, I look at the boxes in the room and think about the many others needing to be built. Luckily, the living room and kitchen had been set up by Uncle Atti. Without him, I would be worrying about organizing the first floor. Instead, I only have to focus on my room, Blake's room and Alice's room. Then we can add to the house as needed.

"Little One, you grew up in a Palace with maids. Why did you think it would be a good idea to try and build furniture—alone?" Atticus asks, amusement on his face.

"Because I thought it wouldn't be hard." With a growl of frustration, I pull away from him and make my way out of what is to be my bedroom and down the stairs. My destination is the kitchen for a glass of wine.

"Wine doesn't fix everything, Crystalline." Atticus states, trailing behind me as I reach the wine cooler built into the wall and take out a one-hundred-year-old red. Pouring two glasses, I hand one to the sassy vampire then take a sip from the other. Of course he is right, wine does not fix anything, but a drink does help calm me down.

"How about I help you build the furniture and then we can go out for dinner? I could use a rare steak." He suggests, the idea tempting.

"Deal. But can we start with the kids' rooms first? I would like them to come home to their own rooms completed after the life they have lived." I agree, smiling as I think about what reactions Blake and Alice will have.

"Definitely." With that, we clink our glasses together and head back upstairs, Atticus bringing the open bottle of wine with us. Next move, I will definitely pay for someone else to deal with all the furniture building.

◆◆◆

"So, you have never been to The Keg?" Atticus chuckles, sipping on his third glass of wine mixed with blood. When he first ordered the drink upon arriving, I had been confused, unsure if this is a normal thing to order in the city. But then Atticus explained to me that this branch is owned by his friend, also a Vampire like him, and that his drink is a secret menu item made especially for vampires trying to blend in with the humans.

"I have only been to allied packs of Alexander's. I spent most of my life in the palace." I explain, munching on the warm bread the waitress left for us to enjoy. The scent of melted butter and cheese on a soft sourdough tantalizes me and causes my stomach to grumble. I cannot wait for my food to be brought to the table.

"So how long will you be in Toronto?" I sigh at this question, turning to look out the window at the people passing by. Some days I wish I were human, being able to enjoy a mundane life without the hassle of a brother who has tried to kill me as an infant and who is actively wanting me dead. To have to prepare myself for a war and take back my rightful inheritance.

"A couple of years. I have to work on making allies and train a little longer before I can return to the north to claim my throne." A gentle hand on mine has me turning to face Atticus, his burgundy eyes warm and inviting and reminding me I am not alone here in my temporary home.

"Well, when you decide to move, let me know. I want to be a part of your life from now on." His warm words has tears filling my eyes and I squeeze his hand as a response, too emotional to express my gratitude to this uncle of mine. Thankfully, our waitress has the perfect timing and places an eighteen ounce steak in front of me. Grinning like the Cheshire cat, I dig into the perfectly cooked beef while Atticus brings up the topic of school for the pups.

We both agreed that a human school will be perfect for them, a place with children their age without the werewolf community around them. After years of abuse, I will have to work on easing Alice and Blake back into the werewolf community with hopes of training the two to control their emotions and their shifts when the time comes.

We talk about Nightmare Moon and what Geminie, Amberle, and the Temple of the Moon Goddess are doing about it as the Royal Pack refuses to step in, which led to a spiralling list of illegal activities coming to surface that have been hidden because of Alexander.

By the end of the meal, I felt angry for not paying attention to the forced mating, the trafficking of she-wolves to human Hunters, and the many Rogues being captured and sold as slaves.

"When the time comes, will you help me change the werewolf laws? I need to provide a safe space for my people, including a way to quickly put the Soulless out of their misery so that they can reincarnate to a better life." Voicing out my thoughts, I close my eyes to calm the rage inside me. The need to kill Alexander so strong that I feel myself on the verge of shifting.

"Of course, Crystalline. We can work together while you are in Toronto to piece together those laws and how to execute them once you become Queen." With a sigh of relief, I open my eyes to see my uncle staring at me with pride, the feeling of the shift receding as my anger settles.

"Why don't we get going? I am sure Alice and Blake are on their way home and will want to see their rooms." Atticus suggests, flagging down our waitress and settling the bill before we head out and make our way to the parking garage. The streets are crowded, the bustling city full of life with different people, leaving me in awe. I feel like a tourist, still in disbelief that Toronto is my home now. And then the scent of blood—werewolf blood—hits me, causing me to stumble. Atticus is quick to catch me, his fangs slightly showing as he too smells it in the air.

"Rogue?" He asks and I nod, closing my eyes to focus on the scent and locate where the smell of blood is coming from. There are multiples of victims, the scents of at least three Rogues being so strong it makes my eyes water.

"We need to see where the blood is coming from. Can you drive while I direct us?" I ask, Atticus nodding in agreement as he does his best to hide his fangs from the view of the humans. In silence, we rush to the garage, me throwing my keys to Atticus and climbing into the passenger seat as he puts the vehicle into drive.

"Right at the exit." I state, making sure all windows are open. Eyes closed, I cling to my moonstone, feeling the magic strengthening my senses.

"Left in three hundred metres."

"Right at the next turn then straight for five hundred."

"Left, right here." I continue to navigate, the smell growing stronger until a scent trail appears in my mind. Sometimes it will fade away and we will have to wait a few minutes until the scent reappears again, until finally we find ourselves parked behind a shady looking warehouse. The scent of blood, wolves and dogs is so strong that I have to cover my nose with a bandana to breathe.

"Where are we?" I ask, seeing a grim look on Atticus' face as we climb out of the vehicle.

"The heart of Little Portugal. Most of the Hunters hide in small communities like Little Italy, Little Portugal and Chinatown. I have a feeling we have just arrived at one of their hideouts." I frown, the scent that has been haunting me strengthening once again as a warehouse garage door opens and a body is thrown out onto the hard pavement.

"Just leave this mutt out there. He is going to be dead anyway." A voice shouts from inside, ordering the two that just threw out what looks to be a large dog.

"I mean, we can always skin his pelt and sell it on the black market." One of the men chuckles, the trailer door closing right away. Without a second thought, I rush towards the body, the scent of rogue wolf strong. Before me lays a black wolf, his body covered in wounds both old and new and a collar burning into his throat. I gasp, ready to kneel beside him and assess his injuries when Atticus pulls me back, keeping his body between me and this Rogue.

"You can't just rush in!" He hisses, his eyes trained on the barely breathing body.

"He needs my help, Uncle!" I argue back, trying to move around the unmoving immortal.

"And you need to learn not to be so reckless!" He growls, placing his hands on my shoulders and stopping me in my place.

"Then help me help him!" My eyes are trained on the wolf as I plead with the vampire before me. I know he is scared to lose me, the daughter his best friend never got to raise, the niece he has been searching for all these centuries, but I cannot just stand there while a werewolf slowly dies.

"Fine. I will go fold the back seats down and we can shove this Rogue in through the trunk. But do not go near him!" Finally, my Uncle concedes before zipping away to where we left the Hummer. I count to five, making sure he is busy before turning back to the wolf and rushing to his side

"I'm here to help!" I coo softly, kneeling behind him so that if this injured wolf were to attack, I can doge quickly. The black wolf lets out a growl, his deep brown eyes glaring at me as blood seeps out from the corner of his lips.

"Oh shush. You're going to die if I don't help." I sigh, placing my hand gently on his flank. He snaps at me, but I am quick to move my hands and grab his muzzle with ease, the anger and hatred evident in the wolf before me.

"Either I help you or you die. Choose." I growl back, allowing my eyes to glow silver. I watch as he thinks over my words, realizing that I only have a moment before Atticus returns when I hear the start of the engine to my Hummer. But finally the growls subside and the wolf lowers his head some what submissively, allowing me to do what I can to save him.

With a sigh of relief, I gently smooth the fur away from some of the wounds, bending down to gently sniff at them and feeling confident that I can help this wolf heal when no scent of poison is present. Now onto the biggest problem, the silver collar.

The skin below it is burned away, the scarring unable to heal with constant contact. Without a second thought, I rush to find a way to remove it, jumping back when the wolf winces and snarls.

"I'm sorry, but try to relax, please. Silver doesn't burn me and I can remove it quickly from you." I explain, slowly moving around so that the wolf can see me. Kneeling once again, this time by his muzzle, I wait for the wolf to trust me and quickly get to work on removing the collar when he gives a slight nod. He growls as I work my fingers around the metal but does not attempt to attack me anymore.

Finally, with a loud click the collar opens and I am able to remove the metal from his neck.

"I thought I said to stay away from him!" Atticus growls out as he backs the Hummer with the trunk open towards us.

"And I thought I did not agree to that!" I argue back, gently running my fingers through the wolf's fur. His breathing has even out but his brown eyes glare at my Uncle.

"You can trust him. He and I are going to bring you away from here." I assure him, bringing his attention to me. I see the internal battle in his eyes, the wolf at least six feet in length from snout to tail debating on if he can believe me or not. I guess his decision is taking too long as Atticus takes the silver collar from my hand using a silk handkerchief and throws it into a dumpster before returning and hauling the black wolf into the Hummer without a second thought then throws me into the passenger seat before zipping to the drivers side and speeding away from the warehouse just in time for the doors to open again and two men walk out, cursing that the black wolf they disposed of is now gone.

"Just like your father, always wanting to save the Damned." He mutters angrily and I smile, leaning onto his shoulder and placing a kiss on that flawless cheek of his.

"Thank you, Uncle."

Chapter 15 – Albot the Rogue

"So why can't we go into the garage?" Blake asks, his bright eyes shifting to the door that leads to the garage. I sigh, scooping a large portion of rice and steak slices into a bowl for the new guest in my home before scooping out some food for Blake and Alice.

"Because Crystalline decided to save a Rogue used in a dog fighting operation last night." Atticus chimes in, his fingers flying across his laptop. Since returning home and spending all night last night and most of the day, my uncle has not left his seat at the breakfast bar while I tended to the Rogue, making sure he made it through the night alive. He is relentlessly trying to get to the bottom of the illegal wolf-fighting ring and help save those Rogues being abused for the amusement of Hunters. I glare at him, not liking the monotone voice he uses to answer Blake, before turning to smile at the pups and bringing a glass of orange juice each to them.

"You both already know I am the Lost Princess, I explained it to you on our drive to Toronto." I start, watching them both nod.

"So because of this, it is my duty to help the wolves in need. The Rogue needed me to help him, and so I helped him." I explain, watching as Alice accepts my answer while Blake mulls it over before eventually accepting my explanation as well. Smiling, I ruffle his hair, happy with the progress Blake and I have made. I hope that soon he will come to trust me without having to second guess if my words are honest or not.

"Uncle Atti, keep the kids away from the garage, please." I ask as I collect the food and a few cold water bottles for the Rogue in my garage, my uncle just waving his hand dismissively.

"You know I will, darling. They listen better than you do, anyway." He answers with a sigh. I roll my eyes at his words, deciding that I will have to play the cute niece card later for not listening to him and going near that Rogue last night. But I just had to get that silver collar off of him so the healing process could start.

Making sure that the pups promise to stay in the house, I leave them in the kitchen to eat and make my way to the garage door just inside the entry way, dodging a few boxes that still need to be carried upstairs. Opening the door slowly, I pause when a low warning growl greets me.

"It's me. I brought food and water." I call out gently, waiting for the growling to stop before entering. With the door firmly shut behind me, I lock it so that the pups can't follow and slowly walk towards the injured black wolf, his brown eyes following my every step.

"It's not much, just some rice and steak but I don't want you to over eat while you are healing." I explain, settling the bowl of food in front of him. He sniffs it, giving me a curious look before taking a tentative bite. I smile, glad to see this wolf trusting me as I sit on the cold concrete, placing the second bowl down and filling it with fresh water from the unopened water bottles. He watches me as he eats, letting me push the water towards him as he takes a deep sip.

"I hope you are feeling a little bit better. It took me all night to make sure you didn't die. You have some nasty wounds on you that made helping you hard." I sigh out, brining my knees to my chest and waiting for the wolf to finish. I want to take a brush to his fur, to help smooth it out and comb out the knots for him. To take him for a bath and help clean all the wounds. But I need to gain his trust first.

"Would you mind if I shift?" I ask, wondering if having another wolf lay near him will help quicken the healing process. He eyes me, his distrust evident as he thinks over my words. After a few moments pass, he nods his approval and I smile. Slowly getting up, I make my way towards the other side of the garage behind a few boxes, removing my clothes including my necklace and placing them just outside the protection of this makeshift wall so that the Rogue can see.

Then I shift. My bones realign themselves quickly and within seconds I re-emerge and carefully trot towards the Rogue. A look of shock is on his face as he realizes I am a runt, barely four feet in length compared to his six feet long wolf, and I can see him softening towards me. Once I am three feet away, I slowly lie down, careful to inch my way forward until I feel his tongue flick across my forehead.

Looking up in surprise, I see his deep brown eyes studying me for a moment, before he motions me to come closer, and so I do. I carefully move until I am lying beside him, his large fluffy tail coming to cover my body as he settles his head across my neck.

The Rogue accepted me and I can't help the happy feeling that has my tail wagging gently. Feeling content, I close my eyes.

◆◆◆

The feeling of someone grooming me wakes me from my slumber and I open my eyes to see the Rogue move his head just in time to avoid an accidental head but from me. Wagging my tail, I move my muzzle to gently lick his cheek, seeing him look away quickly. I have a feeling that he is blushing.

Carefully untangling myself from him, I stretch, motioning to my clothes to indicate I am going to shift, before running behind my makeshift wall again and allowing my body to change back into my skin form and quickly dress. Returning to the Rogue, I see he is standing, his legs a little shaky but smile as I realize he almost reaches my five-foot-five frame with the tip of his ears just below my chin.

"Do you want to go for a shower and clean your wounds?" I ask, walking over and gently scratching behind his left ear. He closes his eyes and lets out a noise of content before nodding his head and I smile.

[Are the pups in bed?] I link my uncle.

[Yes, why?] Atticus replies quickly.

[I am bringing the Rogue inside for a shower.] I can tell my uncle wants to protest, but I shut off the connection before he can go on lecturing me and slowly walk towards the garage door, unlocking it and opening the wooden door to see an extremely disappointed vampire staring at me.

"Hi." I cheerfully greet, feeling the rogue behind me look past my body.

"Don't "hi" me, young wolf! You know I disapprove of this." My uncle hisses, his burgundy eyes set in a grim stare. I sigh, motioning to the Rogue to calm down when he starts to bare his teeth before looking back at my uncle.

"His wounds are dirty and he needs to be cleaned up to heal. He trusts me and I trust him." I state. Silence passes over us and I wait as my hard headed uncle stares between the rogue and I before finally sighing and backing away.

"Fine. But he uses the guest room down here, and I will be outside the door in case he tries anything." Atticus relents and I smile, rushing forwards and giving him a hug.

"Thank you for trusting me, Uncle Atti." He sighs, wrapping his arms around me and hugging me back, placing a quick kiss on my temple.

"Go help clean that Rogue. I will find some clothes for him." With that, my uncle zips away and I motion for the black wolf to follow me to the guest room.

Opening the door, I walk towards the attached bath and for once am happy I have a large tub for this room, knowing that the wolf might have a hard time fitting into anything smaller than the jacuzzi in the guest room or in my room – I did not want him in my room.

The wolf watches my movements as I set the temperature, making sure to keep it warm before motioning him forward as I fill the tub for him to soak in.

"I am going to give you some privacy so that you can shift and take the time to clean yourself. I have some medicine that I can apply to your wounds when you are ready." I see him staring at me, appreciation in his eyes as he walks forward and nuzzles my body in thanks.

I smile, gently running my fingers through his fur, wondering what this wolf will look like, happy that I had rescued him last night. With a gentle movements, I give the wolf a hug, mentioning that my uncle will be back with clothes soon, and make my way out of the room and to the kitchen where I get started on preparing food and taking out some medicinal tonics Ira sent me last week to help heal this wolf.

I listen intently to the room down the hall, wincing as the wolf shifts painfully and as he tries to hold back his screams. It seems like he has not shifted for years and my heart breaks for him.

"I thought you were going to help him bathe." Atticus says quietly, leaning against the entrance with a bag in his hand.

"He needs some privacy and I am in no mood of cleaning a fully grown man." I state, taking a cool bag of blood from the mini fridge and throwing it at my uncle. He chuckles, taking a straw and stabbing it into the bag like a juice box before taking a sip and looking down the hall.

"You just didn't want to wash his man bits." He teases, making me blush while I focus on making a medicinal meal with vegetables, rice and the tonics.

"You're wrong." Is the only argument I can come up with.

"I am right." He counters before zipping away, most likely to bring the clothes to the rogue. I sigh, my hand reaching to clasp the moonstone around my neck as I think about what he said. How I did not want to touch the wolf intimately.

The truth is he is right. Being rejected made me realize I am not ready to face any males. Minutes pass, and with the meal ready, I make my way towards the guest room to see how my uncle and the Rogue are, making it to the door just as a stabbing pain runs through me.

Falling to my knees, I suppress a scream and tears run down my eyes and wonder what this is. Wonder how I can be feeling this pain when I have not been injured.

"What's wrong with her?" Strong arms scoop me close to a sturdy chest, the scent of pine and snow calming my mind.

"She was rejected by her mate. That bastard must be fucking some whore." Atticus replies with a hiss, tucking his hand under my chin and having me look into his eyes.

"Make it stop!" I plead through teary eyes, feeling like death is clawing at me.

"Rogue-" He starts, looking away.

"Albot. My name is Albot."

"Fine, Albot. I am going to compel her. So don't go attacking me." Atticus sighs out before retuning his gaze to mine. I bite down on my lip, the pain growing and making me want to scream but I have the pups to worry about. I can't scare them.

"Crystalline, look into my eyes." His voice is smooth, silky and his burgundy eyes glow a bright red. He captures my attention, the scream dying as my mind goes blank.

"Good. You are going to sleep, Young One, allow your body to rest. When the pain is gone, you will awaken." As if on cue, my eyes close and darkness takes over as the pain fades away.

Chapter 16 – Trust

I groan as consciousness seeps in, my body sore for some unknown reason and the scent of pine and snow wrapping around me. I question if someone had slipped a drug in my drink until the events of last night flood into my mind. Panicking, I bolt upright, looking around to see that I am in the guest room and that a male with black hair and tanned skin lays beside me, his deep brown eyes watching my every move. Something about those eyes seem familiar until I remember that he was the Rogue I saved.

"Uh, hi." I mumble. Running my hand through my hair.

"Good morning. How are you feeling?" His deep voice is captivating, holding the ruggedness of a man that should be living deep in the woods. I suppress the shiver that runs down my spine and stop myself from thinking of how attractive this man is.

"Sore. Did we—"

"No. While you were helping me, you almost collapsed in pain. That Vampire of yours said something about your mate being with another female." The man answers and I nod. Amberle and Geminie warned me that if Narin messes around with another female or I with another male, then we would each feel a severe stabbing pain. I remember the pain from last night, the being held in this wolf's arms and Uncle Atti compelling me. Then I woke up here.

"So, how did we end up in the same bed?" I ask, getting a chuckle from the one beside me.

"Well, some little unconscious she-wolf wouldn't let go of her death grip on me even in her sleep so the vampire—"

"His name is Atticus." I correct, not liking how this wolf calls my uncle Vampire.

"Atticus conceded in allowing you to sleep in this room with me. I have a feeling he may be listening in right now."

"That he is." The door opens and Atticus walks in, a glass of orange juice in hand as he comes and settles on my side of the bed, a look of concern on his face.

"Are you okay, Little One?" He asks, handing me the cold drink and cupping my cheek.

"I am." I reassure him, taking a long sip of the much-needed cool orange juice. I can feel a pair of eyes on me as I look from the corner of my eyes to see this wolf staring at Atticus and I with confusion.

"To think a wolf can be in the same room as a vampire without him taking a drink." He mumbled under his breath. I pause my sipping, bringing the glass down and stare at this wolf in confusion.

"What do you mean?" I ask, worried about what he said. If vampires are part of the reason he was in a state of near death, then Atticus and I need to put a stop to the Hunter's den.

"What I mean is I have seen plenty of vampires come and go in that warehouse you found me in. All men." He answers, his brown eyes becoming hard with anger as he sits up and looks out the window.

"They make a deal with the Hunters and bring in Rogues they capture in exchange to get the chance to fuck a she-wolf and drink from her. Most times, the raped she-wolf is bled dry." He continues, horror filling me. I look to Uncle Atticus, seeing his own dark eyes darken further as his fangs protrude. I can feel his anger and watch as he gets up and start pacing.

"I heard rumors. But I never thought it was this bad. I need to contact Ira." My uncle states. Feeling left out, I climb to my feet and step into my uncle's path, stopping his pacing.

"Rumors about what?" I demand, my eyes glowing silver with anger at what I just heard.

"A werewolf's blood is like acid to a vampire. Add in pleasure, and it's like steroids." The Rogue answers instead. I gasp, looking back to my uncle who nods confirming that what was just said is true.

"How has no one stopped this before?" I ask, finding my legs growing weak with shock as I sit back on the bed.

"Blame the Royals. King Alexander has his hand in this." The Rogue scoffs. I stiffen, my eyes meeting my uncle's who motions me to come to him. I can feel the hate for the Royals rolling off of this rogue and part of me is scared. He is weak from the wounds but I know that in a fight, it will be hard to tell who will come out alive.

[Crystalline, we need to get you away from him.] My uncle links me. I close my eyes and think about this, think about if this Rogue will turn on me if I tell him the truth. But if I lie, I may lose a potential ally.

[Can you let me explain things to him first? If he attacks, I won't blame you for killing him.] I link back, opening my eyes to silently plead with Atticus. I see the turmoil in his eyes as he begins pacing again. I know that he is considering my words and when he lets out a sigh, I smile.

[Fine. But one hostile move, and I end him.]

[Thank you.] I slowly turn in the bed, looking at the wolf only to find him looking at me. He eyes me, but the distrust from before is gone and I am happy for that. But now comes the hard part.

"Can I know your name?" I ask, wanting to break the ice between us.

"Albot Everrette. And may I know yours?" Albot answers, a soft smile on his face. I take a deep breath, feeling nervous and looking back to Atticus. He nods, letting me know he trusts me and has my back before I look back at Albot.

"It's Crystalline." I state quietly.

"Crystalline Thorn." I watch as shock, then disbelief and anger fill Albot's handsome face. I shrink, trying to make myself look smaller than I am as the Rogue jumps off the bed and away from me.

"You're HIS daughter?" He growls accusingly. I look up, angry at the accusation and ready to yell back, but Atticus places a hand on my shoulder and stops me.

"Actually, she is the Lost Princess and the true heir to the throne." Atticus states. Albot scoffs, crossing his arms over his chest and I look away, not wanting to gawk at the muscles that ripple under the black cotton t-shirt he is wearing.

"You expect me to believe that? Everyone knows that the Lost Princess is most likely dead." Albot retorts, his anger towards me - towards royals - crashing into my body like waves and making me shiver.

"Well, I am not. I was saved by Goddess Morai, and it wasn't until eighteen years ago that the protective magic faded and my adoptive mother Queen Clarice found me." I yell back, unable to stay silent. I glare at Albot, not wanting to back down from this wolf who I just saved. He can be mad at Alexander for having a hand with the Hunters, but he cannot be mad at me when I risked my own life to save him two nights ago.

"If this is true, then prove it. Royals can share memories, so share yours with me." Albot challenges. Taken aback, I think about his words for a moment before climbing over the bed and marching to him. Without hesitation, I grab the back of his head and pull his forehead to mine until they touch and close my eyes. I allow the power in my blood to flow out and with it, my memories of the last two months flood into Albot's mind.

Everything from the rejection to the dreamscape with my father, to the chat with Amberle, Geminie, Ira, Dominic and Ariven. How I trained with everyone and read books. I even showed him the memory of the restricted area and what happened when I touched the moonstone. When all the memories have been sent, including how I found and saved him, I back away and fall onto the bed, my energy spent.

"Believe me now, asshole?" I growl out, Atticus coming to support me and hand me my half-finished glass of orange juice that I happily chug.

"I... Wow... A princess saved me." In awe of what he has just been shown, Albot slides down the wall and onto the floor. I chuckle and nod, the hostility in the room disappearing.

"That's right, this idiot I call my niece risked herself to save you. She plans to take back her throne and fix the shitshow Alexander has created the last hundred years." Atticus agrees, a smirk on his lips.

"Then count me in. I would love to see that smug bastard's face when his heart is ripped out." I smile, the soft look in Albot's eyes returning as he looks at me. I can see that Atticus is warming up to the rogue and for some reason I get the feeling that Albot will be someone special to me.

"How about we order in breakfast? I bet the pups would love to meet Albot over Denny's breakfast." I suggest, looking up at Atticus who smiles.

"I will call Heidi and have her make a stop at Denny's on her way over. She has the files you asked her to look into about the Witch Avilla." Atticus agrees, placing a kiss on my forehead before zipping away. Now left in the room alone with Albot, I can see his curious gaze on me.

"Pups? As in the ones you saved?"

"Yes, Alice and Blake. Blake might be standoffish, but he will warm up to you eventually. Alice... she has this ability to sense the good in people. I plan to ask Ira about it when I go to the Temple with them before school." Albot nods at my answer, pushing himself off the ground and walking towards me. When he comes to stand before me, he holds out his hand. Hesitating, I look up at his eyes, the brown orbs full of trust and loyalty, something I did not expect after three days. With a smile, I place my hand in his and feel his fingers wrap around mine. My hand is so small in his but it feel so natural, like they were meant to fit in his grasp.

"It's nice to meet you, darling." He whispers, his husky voice low and deep. I shiver, letting his scent wrap around me as I feel a connection, a pack connect, build between us.

"It's nice to meet you too Albot."

Chapter 17 - City Rogues

"Alice, Blake, time for breakfast." I yell up the stairs for the two pups. Two years have passed since we have made this house our home. Since we came to Toronto and met Atticus. Two years of them slowly working on shedding their past and looking to their future working with Hailey every week and reminding the siblings that they are safe. With a smile, I make my way back to the kitchen, Albot sitting at the breakfast bar reading the paper as Atticus works on his laptop as usual.

"When are we going to tell them?" Albot asks, setting the paper down and joining me at the stove to swipe a piece of bacon from the plate.

"Later tonight. I want to take them out today to go apple picking like we always do." I sigh, swatting away his hand as Albot tries to sneak another bacon off of the plate. I glare at him in warning, evading his out stretched hand as I move towards the breakfast bar where a spread of food is waiting just in time for a now-sixteen-year-old Blake and a twelve-year-old Alice to run in. I chuckle, watching the two put together plates of food before joining Atticus, eyeing his cup full of red liquid.

"Blood as usual, Uncle Atti?" Alice asks before taking a bite of her pancake.

"Nope, cranberry juice this time." He chuckles out a reply, turning the laptop towards the children.

"Blake, since you just turned sixteen four months ago and got your G1 driver's licence, Crystalline gave me permission to take you car shopping." He exclaims, a look of pride in the vampire's eyes.

[A car, really?] I smile at Albot as he links me, nodding my head in response. Turning my attention back to my pups, I watch as Blake rushes around the table to Atticus, giving the man a hug as he thanks him happily and begins to look at the laptop with him. It seems like these two will have a fun day planned.

"I hope you saved some food for me!" Turning to the opened back door, I smile at Marcie as she kicks off her sneakers and places a basket I have no doubt is filled with fruits and berries from our garden. To think a year ago this she-wolf was sent to capture me by Alexander. She had managed to track me down out in the Altona Forest as I took a chance to run through the trees one night. Marcie had managed to catch me off guard, her brown wolf blending in with nature when she tackled me.

Of course, I won the fight and every so often when I needed a run, I would run into her. We became rivals, my small form and training with Amberle giving me an edge over her slightly larger brown wolf form. With respect, we soon started communicating in human form when she could track me down in the city, knowing full well she could not attack me in plain views of human due to the secrecy laws.

It wasn't until she was captured by Hunters that we became friends. I had gotten used to seeing this Latina every few days that when I went two weeks without seeing her, I began to worry and asked Atticus to help locate the she-wolf who was sent to take me back to the Royal Pack.

Within moments, we located her in the same Hunters' den we saved Albot from. It was all the evidence Uncle Atti needed to take this place down, and with the help of Geminie, Amberle and the Acolytes from the Temple of the Goddess, we were able to take down the Hunters and save many Rogues from the horrors of the illegal dogfighting ring.

Sadly, Marcie was found by me and Albot barely breathing. I spent days tending to her comatose form, trying to keep this she-wolf alive, until one day she woke up. After realizing her target had found and saved her, she devoted her loyalty to me as the next Queen and cut contact with Alexander, joining my misfit family here in Toronto.

"There is always breakfast for you, Marcie." I laugh, the Latina coming in and giving me a hug before rushing to fill her own plate, just as Albot hands me a plate filled with pancakes and bacon, his brown eyes looking at me warmly. I thank him, deciding to lean on the counter while Alice chimes in about what Blake's car should have including heated seats and Bluetooth on the list and I enjoy the small happy atmosphere.

"You guys tell them yet?" Marcie asks, joining Albot and I by the counter.

"Not yet. I want to take them apple picking at Spirit Tree first, let them enjoy the day before they have to be told." I answer before taking a bite of bacon.

"Are you nervous? It's been two years since you left wolf country. Now you'll be forming a pack of your own to take down the Royal Pack." She continues after my answer, giving me a small smile. I sigh, placing my plate still half full on the counter, my mood shifting with this conversation.

"Albot and I have been training for two years with Atticus, the wolves of Bloodmoon and the wolves from Silver Crystal Crescent. I have even gone to see Ira alone at the temple to get some personal training. The only other step now is to form a pack and take back my throne." I answer Marcie, feeling Albot wrap his arm around me and pull me to his side. Since the first night I felt the disrespect to the mate bond and Narin fucked another wolf, Albot has become my confidant and best friend.

It did take a small argument between us to come to an understanding the morning after being compelled to sleep by my uncle and weeks of getting used to another wolf with Alpha blood in the house, but we soon became inseparable, almost like a couple to the humans who we deal with in our lives here in the city. Albot may be six years older than me, but the care he has given to me even after the years he spent abused by Hunters makes me appreciate this heavily tattooed six-foot-seven wolf.

"So, you are nervous." Marcie teases and I groan, turning to hide my face into Albot's chest with a mumbled 'yes.' A deep chuckle comes from the chest I am hiding in, Albot rubbing my back gently as Marcie gags, probably sick of the public display of affection in front of her.

"You okay, mama?" Alice calls out, causing me to turn and look at the twelve year old.

"I'm fine. Marcie is just being a brat to me." I reassure her, giving a playful glare to my friend who nudges me with he elbow.

"A brat, huh?" She growls out playfully and I smile, bumping my shoulder with hers. I chuckle, leaning into her and resting my head on her shoulder.

"Yes, a brat." With that, we continue eating our breakfast before I announce to Blake and Alice that we will be heading to their favourite place today, and rush to get dressed before we miss out on apple picking.

"So, do I need to get the moving company called in?" Atticus calls out once the pups are out of ear shot. I shudder, thinking back to the nightmare of having to put furniture together two years ago. Thankfully, I had my uncle, and then Albot, to help put all the furniture together within a few days.

"Not yet. We still have a week before we need to leave." Sitting next to my Uncle, I lean into his arm and close my eyes. I have gotten so used to his scent of mint and raspberry with a hint of iron that I will end up missing it when we leave Toronto. But all things change and I cannot be a city Rogue forever if I am to take down Coro and Alexander and take the throne back.

"That and we still need a place to come visit you, Atticus." Albot chimes in, getting a chuckle out of my uncle.

"You know. As much as I hated my niece putting herself in danger to save you, I am glad she did."

❖❖❖

I chuckle while recording Blake trying his best to reach for a large apple above his head, the bright red fruit looking enticing to all of us. But my pup seems to have forgotten that even though he is sixteen and has shifted, he is still in need of a growth spurt. With a frustrated growl, I watch as he slowly backs up before taking a running leap and finally manages to grab the fruit in triumph.

We all cheer and chuckle while I turn to see Albot lifting Alice to help her pick a yellow golden delicious apple that has caught her eye. It seems like taking the pups here to enjoy some fresh country air mixed with the sweet scent coming off of the fruit and pick apples from our favourite spot was the right thing to do.

"So, what are we going to do with all these apples?" Marcie asks and I shrug, accepting the hot apple cider my friend brings me from the bar to the left of the property.

"Apple pie, apple bread, applesauce. Just depends on what we can make before we leave." I answer, sipping on the hot drink while I show the video of Blake's success in grabbing the apple minutes earlier. We walk around the orchard, Albot becoming Alice's helper in gathering the apples up high that catches the twelve year old's eyes while Marcie and I enjoy the comfortable silence between us.

"Are we getting pizza?" Alice asks as she bounds over with a smile, Albot trailing behind her with arms full of bags filled with different types of apples.

"Did Albot say we are getting pizza?" I ask in return, seeing the grin growing on her face.

"Yes!" She shouts, making me wince as I chuckle.

"Then I guess we are getting pizza." I confirm, getting a squeal of delight. Blake bounds over soon after, his two bags filled as well and I inform him of dinner plans, getting a fist bump in return. With our apples picked, we head back towards the farm shoppe and pay for the apples. Albot and Blake bring the bags to my Hummer while Alice, Marcie and I head inside, the smell of the wood fire oven hitting us the moment we step inside.

"Hey Crys, did you get some apples?" Cara calls out from the cash as soon as she sees us, a smile on my friend's face.

"Yeah, Albot is bringing them to the car now with Blake. What's the featured pizza today?" I smile as the blonde-haired person comes to join us, an order form and a pen in hand as Marcie and Alice takes a cart, ready to fill it with goodies and cider.

"ABC Pizza. It has Apples, Bacon and Cheddar on it." She answer. I smile, the feature sounding like a great idea.

"I will take three of those, plus two Spirit Trees extra goat cheese, and a Wise Guy then." She takes down my order and began taking it to the kitchen just as Albot and Blake walk in, Albot wrapping his arms around me and placing a kiss on my temple.

"Are the pizzas ordered?" Albot asks, followed by the sounds of Cara yelling "Ordering" from the kitchen entrance.

"Does that answer your question." I chuckle, the two of us walking around slowly. Marcie comes by with the cart, the poor thing already filled with granola, cheese, cider and fresh produce. We quickly make our way to the freezers, deciding to buy a few packs of burgers and entrees while we wait for four 'o'clock to come around and we can get our pizza. Alice is attracted by a bracelet made with moonstone and opal; her bright eyes unable to look away from it. Taking it off the display, I bring it to the cash register, adding it to our haul and paying. The moment the bracelet is paid for, I hand it to the little pup, seeing her happily place it on her left wrist before hugging and thanking me for the gift. The order is called and I Albot goes to grab the six pizzas while Marcie takes the pups to the car to store our goods in the trunk.

"This might be our last time visiting for a while. We are moving up north next week." I tell Cara as the two of us chat, getting a hug from my friend.

"Well, when you are down in this area, come by for a visit." She sighs out, giving me a smile. I promise to visit when I am down in Toronto visiting my uncle before saying goodbye and heading to the car with Albot. The one thing I am really going to miss is this little farm shoppe. Climbing into the passenger side of my vehicle, I take the pizzas from Albot so that he can drive us home.

"After dinner, we have something to tell you pups." Albot says, turning to look at Blake and Alice.

"Is it something bad?" Alice asks, worry in her little voice.

"No, it might be a good thing. But I promise we will all stay together." I reassure the little girl. With that, the Hummer is put into drive and we make our way home.

Chapter 18 – Moving Back to Wolf Country

"Are you sure everything is packed up?" Atticus asks, his burgundy eyes filled with concern as he looks over every detail of the house we are saying goodbye to. Today is the day we leave to where the new pack will be, Alice and Blake excited to return to the forest and be a part of a proper pack that will treat them with respect. These last two years in the city has been good for all of us, especially when we would leave for summers with Bloodmoon or Silver Crystal Crescent to train.

"Yes. Everything we will need is packed with us. Even the new furniture we plan to build once there. Ira even has a witch coming to help set up a secured pack line for us to prevent humans from wandering in if they aren't mated to a supernatural." I reassure the worrying vampire, wrapping my arms around him and giving him a long hug. I did not want to leave my uncle behind, I even offered to have him come live in the pack with us but his home and life is in Toronto.

"I just don't want to see you go young wolf." He whispers, burying his face in my hair and taking in my scent.

"I know, Uncle Atti, but I need to. When you visit, there will be a cozy cabin with internet access waiting for you this Christmas." He chuckles at my words, pulling away to look at me with pride. I smile up at him, trying my hardest to fight back tears. This man took me under his wing, worked with me as we thought of fair laws for the werewolf nation for when I reclaimed my throne, took me to meet powerful Alphas that agreed to be my allies.

When we were relaxing, he traveled with me to see all of Canada, took me to Europe and Japan to meet the packs that were at the Alliance Ball the day I was rejected to create alliances with them. He taught me to fight vampires while Heidi taught me to fight witches and how to scent out spells and chams by dark and light witches.

They made me powerful and helped shaped me, Blake, Alice, Albot and Marcie into strong wolves capable of anything.

"Don't forget, Heidi and I are getting married in spring. You have to come down to walk me down the aisle." He reminds me, fighting back his own tears and making us both laugh.

"Don't worry Uncle Atti, I will be there and so will the others." With a final hug, he walks me to my Hummer, Alice already inside it with Blake at the wheel. Albot is with his own truck, the vehicle attached to a trailer with our items inside.

"I promise to have your Jeep sent to you, kiddo." Atticus promises Blake, the teen smiling as he leans over to fist bump the vampire.

"I know, Uncle. I can't wait to drive it." I see the sadness in his eyes and sigh. Atticus and Blake became close over the years, the vampire taking Blake under his wing and teaching him about law. I know Blake will work hard to become a lawyer and when the time comes, will train under Atticus at his firm.

"You can always FaceTime Uncle Atti and come down to visit him every summer to intern at his law firm." I remind Blake, sliding into the passenger side and spotting Alice curled up already asleep in the back seat, her arms wrapped around a giant stuffed bunny we won for her at Canada's Wonderland just after arriving to Toronto.

"Your mom is right, kiddo. I'll see you this Christmas with Heidi, and then you can show me the best hunting spots." With that, Atticus closes my door for me, giving me a final kiss on the cheek before we drive off.

◆◆◆

[How far away till we get there?] For the umpteenth time we hear Blake groan through the mind link, glad I had the sixteen year old driving one of the moving trucks with Albot before I could smack the living shit out of him after leaving our motel. It's been five days since we left Toronto, spending nights in motels that back into forest for us to run in wolf form. Of course, the five-day drive meant tensions are high.

[Blake, shut the hell up. We get there when we get there!] And here comes the fighting as Marcie snaps finally. I sigh, rolling my eyes as I wait to see where this fight will lead.

[Bite me, Marcie! You're not the Alpha so you can't boss me around!] Blake retorts and I groan. He is in for a beating from the spitfire Latina when we reach our home.

[Who the hell do you think is her Beta, Blake?]

[Albot, duh!]

[Actually, I am fairly sure Matrix will be her Beta.] Albot cuts in.

[No, he called and says he wants to be in charge of the Warriors.] Marcie retorts.

[So Blake is right, me, then.] Albot sight out nonchalantly.

[Why you, why not me?!]

[Because you would make a better Head Tracker.] I groan again as Albot, Marcie and Blake get into their argument, wanting nothing more than to hit all three of them with a frying pan up side the head. Deciding that the best plan of action is to ignore them, I shut down the link and tune in to my playlist on Spotify. I will deal with the three stooges later when we reach out new home.

I feel so tired from the long hours of driving, being surrounded by trees feels isolating, lonely, and I ever wonder how I managed to live eighteen years in a forest. I miss the hustle and bustle of the city, walking past humans, Rogues, Vampires and Witches on the street. I miss the chatter and the life everyone lived and being able to enjoy so many sounds.

Now, I will have to be deep in the forest, create a strong pack and then head farther North to claim my throne. Will I get used to the isolation again? But I know deep inside I have to do this. To end the tyranny and destruction Alexander and Coro has brought to wolfkind. People need me and I need to be there for them.

This move will also benefit the pups. They need a pack; I can already see Blake being agitated and aggressive without a pack life. Alice will be like that when she first shifts too, edgy and needing the support of a pack.

Looking through the rear-view mirror, I smile at Alice cuddling her rabbit, her focus on the book in her hand as she reads. The little bookworm I have will be excited to see the library I have at the Palace when we move there. Suddenly, the music is cut off with the sound of my ringtone and I frown, clicking the answer button on the steering wheel.

"Crystalline speaking." I answer, wondering why a private caller is calling me when I take a quick look at the dashboard.

"So how long till I get to see you again." My face is split into a grin when I hear Matrix's voice, the last time we talked was two weeks ago when Ira and I decided it is time to move back into wolf country and start a pack.

"Maybe five hours. My pack has been bickering non-stop and I had to shut the link down to avoid a headache." I answer, taking a look at the time and the GPS estimate arrival.

"Sounds like you are having fun." He chuckles and I groan.

"Nope. Quite sure Marcie and Blake want to kill each other right now." My reply brings out another bout of laughter from my friend making me growl. I definitely need to give him a good beating later.

"Look, Crysta, it's a few more hours and then you get to see your new home. I even have a surprise waiting for you."

"Matrix, I hate surprises." I remind my friend.

"Yeah, I know, hence why I always like to make surprises for you. Anyway, I have to go. Our friends are helping with getting the pack house cleaned out and we have a few cabins being finished off."

"Okay, stay safe, Trix. I miss you."

"I miss you too, Crysta." With a sigh I hang up the phone and focus on the driving. I haven't received a call from Albot to open the link back up considering the way they were bickering earlier. If there is an emergency or we need to communicate, he will call my cell phone. For now, I just enjoy the views before me while continuing to my new pack.

◆◆◆

Looking at the GPS I grin and turn to Alice who is sitting munching on a bag of ketchup chips.

"One more hour, then we are home!" I exclaim, seeing a smile on her face.

"I can't wait to run in the forest." She giggles, her eyes scanning the trees as we grow closer to our new home. Turning onto the barely visible dirt road, I check the side mirror to see if the others are following me, thankful when I notice the truck we bought with Blake and Albot inside.

Awwwwooooooooh

A howl sounds in the distance, Alice letting out a whimper of fear as she scoots away from the window to clutch her stuffed rabbit. With a frown, I open up the pack link again.

[Shut it, Marcie!] I call out when I hear Marcie retort to something Blake said. Silence follows as I keep my eyes on the trees before me, wondering if I can sense the owner of the howl.

[Albot, friend or foe?] I aske. With Albot being owned by Hunters for most of his life before Atticus and I rescued him, he is the one with the most knowledge on if a howl is friendly or if we have to fight our way out soon.

[Soulless. It sounds like it is tracking us and reporting to its companions.] My frown deepens, knowing that my brother is the one labelled Soulless King. It doesn't surprise me that he would have his minions tracking me the moment I enter wolf country. But their pursuit will be for nothing as we will reach what will be our new pack in a few minutes. I can feel the power of the barrier created by the witch Cassandra that Ira and Geminie wants me to meet radiating the closer we get.

Something slamming into my car has me pressing the gas pedal harder, zooming away from what ever is trying to knock my car over.

[Albot?] I call out, looking in the mirror once more to see him doing the same.

[Hot on your tail Crystalline with Marcie behind me.] He reassures. Then I feel it. The barrier envelops me, welcoming me in with a warm glow.

[In the clear. Should be smooth driving from here.] His answer soothes me as I pull over to the side of the road, turning the car off and reaching my hand out to Alice. I can see the terror in her eyes, knowing the suffering and fear that Soulless has brought to her life.

"We are safe now, hun. The barrier will keep them out right now." My words are soft whispers as I try my best to calm her down. She clings to my hand, breathing in my scent as we sit in silence for a moment.

[You two okay?] Marcie asks, the other vehicles parking beside us.

[Yeah, Alice is scared because of them. You can drive on ahead and we will be there soon.] I reassure everyone, feeling the unease Blake has with his sister being upset.

[Alice, do you want me to come join you?] He asks. I wait for Alice to answer, letting the little girl choose if she needs her brother.

[No, I have mama and Honey here. You make sure our new home is safe.] Her voice is quiet in the link and I sigh, relieved that this event hasn't ruined the progress we worked so hard for these last two years. Alice clung to Blake for the first five months of living in Toronto, always having a hard time in school with fear of her old pack returning to take her away to be a Breeder. It took months of therapy and taking her out to child-friendly places for her to be able to walk around without Blake by her side.

The others continue on their way once making sure we will be alright, and I pull Alice to sit in the front passenger seat, her stuffed bunny Honey in her arms as we take a moment to relax.

"You ready to go see our new home?" I ask after her breathing evens out and the fear radiating off of her settles.

"Yes!" With that, I turn the Hummer on and continue driving, this time going at a snail's pace for Alice to take in the forest that will be ours to explore.

"It's big!" she exclaims, her wide eyes staring out the window.

"There's also a lake we can swim in and go fishing." Her eyes dart to me and I chuckle, reaching out to ruffle her golden hair. This is the reaction I was hoping for. She no longer is the little pup scared of a shadow. Now, she is a pup excited to run free in the woods like any other werewolf.

Chapter 19 – Pack Astraea

We reach finally reach what will be my new pack house, a three-story Victorian styled building with a large, updated kitchen, offices and a large library on the second floor, and bedrooms for guests on the third. I stare in awe at the magnificent building, the white brick covered in ivy but all the chimneys seem to be clear as smoke puffs from them. This will be my home for another year. Then I will have to pass the title on to someone else once I take back the Royal Pack.

"You made it!" A voice calls out as I exit the vehicle and see Geminie rushing towards me, giving me a hug.

"Yeah. We had a bit of a situation before reaching the boundary." I answer, Alice scurrying over to me with a smile on her face.

"Hi, Gemmy!" She squeals excitedly.

"Hi, Ally-cat!" I chuckle as Alice launches herself into the future Moon Goddess' arms. These two grew close as Geminie figured out Alice can see auras during our first visit to Silver Crystal Crecent, Geminie taking my pup under her wing to train her powers.

"Is Destiny here?" She asks, looking around just in time to see Destiny toddling out of the house hand in hand with Brent while Amberle's twins chase the two toddlers.

"I think that answered your question. Why don't you go play?" I laugh, seeing Alice nod and bolt towards her friends, a smile on her face as if what happened earlier never happened at all.

"So, Rogues?" Dominic asks, walking towards me with Albot and Ariven.

"Soulless, actually. It seems Coro is trying to keep tabs on her." Albot answers instead. I sigh, walking into his open arms and taking in Albot's scent, letting my body relax in his touch.

"Finally! Took you long enough to get here Crysta!" An all too familiar voice calls out, making me pull away from Albot to see a grinning Matrix leaning against a tree not to fare away. It looks like he has just gotten back from a run.

Without a second thought, I bolt towards him, taking a running start to jump into his open arms and wrapping my legs around his waist. A phone call every once in a while for the past two years could never replace feeling my best friend's hug.

I smile, burying my face into the crook of his neck and taking in his scent, tears filling my eyes. I missed him, missed the man that trained me and guarded me my whole life. Missed my best friend who knew all my secrets.

"Welcome home, Crystalline." He whispers, holding me tight to the amusement of our on lockers. But something felt off. There is something that has changed about Matrix that I can't pin point. A change in his scent.

"Get your hands off my mate, you whore!" A shrill voice calls out. Looking around, I notice a she-wolf stalking towards Matrix and I, anger and hatred on her face as she storms towards us. Albot is already by my side, blocking this wolf's attempt to tear me away from Matrix, ruining our reunion. Climbing off of Matrix, I stand in front of my friend protectively, eyeing this wolf before me who is fuming, her eyes glaring daggers at me.

"Maya, this is my friend I told you about. The Alpha we will be following." Matrix explains impatiently, a look of exasperation on his face.

"Even if she is Crystalline, that doesn't mean she can hang off of you when you have a mate you have yet to mark!" Maya screams back, anger clearly filling each word.

[Explain.] I order my friend through our link, our close proximity making it possible to link each other once more.

[Don't trust her, Crystalline. We met a few months ago while I was training and this mate bond snapped into place. But the thing is this bond seems off. Like it's not supposed to be there.] Matrix explains. My guard rises as I stare at this she-wolf, relaying the information to the rest of the wolves. We all eye her suspiciously as she turns to face me, I can already see she wants to tear me apart and I refuse to allow this disrespect any further.

"Listen, you little bitch." I growl out, allowing the power of a Royal wolf to pulsate in my blood and target this weak wolf. I watch as she freezes, her body unable to resist the power of an Alpha Queen.

"I will be your Alpha starting today. I will not take your disrespect nor your unwanted anger, do I make myself clear?" I ask. She does her best to resist, letting out a feral growl towards me. With a growl of my own, the force shaking the trees behind her, I walk over and grab Maya by the throat, slowly choking her. She fights me, her face slowly turning blue as I increase the pressure. I can hear Albot holding back Matrix, the bond making my friend act rashly to protect this so-called mate of his, reassuring Matrix that I will release Maya as soon a she submits.

"Do. I. Make. Myself. Clear?" I ask again, slowly pronouncing each word. Finally, she nods and I release her, watching the annoying she-wolf crumble to the ground as she gasps for much-needed air. The strange thing is, Matrix did not plead for forgiveness for her. He did not beg for me to release her. I could feel my friend tense when I held Maya by the throat, but that was it. With a final look of disdain to the wolf, I turn and walk away from Maya and towards my friends, Albot hot on my heels after reminding Matrix to take care of Maya.

"Now, that's an Alpha!" Amberle exclaims, handing her pup Brent to Dominic before rushing forward and wrapping me in a hug.

"Thanks, I learned from the two best she-wolves I know." With a chuckle, I hug the she-wolf back as Geminie walks towards me with a woman whose hair is as red as blood and eyes as blue as the sky. Something inside me tells me I know this woman, that I have met her before. But I cannot pinpoint where.

"Is... Is this her?" She asks Geminie, her eyes filled with unshed tears.

"This is Crystalline, Cassandra." Geminie confirms. The woman walks towards me and I can feel the magic pulsate off of her—she is a Witch, and a strong one at that. She stops just before me, her eyes scanning my body from head to toe, landing on the moonstone necklace hanging from my neck.

"You look like Luna. And you have the moonstone still." She croaks, tears falling from her eyes.

"You knew my mother?" I ask in disbelief.

"Little pup, I helped her birth you." Cassandra chuckles, her hands pulling me into her arms in a hug. Shocked, I stay still, unable to comprehend what is happening. This Witch was my mother's handmaiden, she helped to birth me and my sister.

"I spent days chanting protection spells onto you and Selene. Days praying to Morai to protect you from Coro. Now here you are, grown up into a beautiful young lady." She continues. Her warmth brings tears to my eyes as a distant lullaby plays in my mind. Without thinking, I wrap my arms around her, closing my eyes and smelling sage and ash on the Witch, a scent that comforted me in my dreams.

"Thank you. You are the reason Coro couldn't kill me as a pup." I whisper. I allow the Witch to hold me, feeling a motherly comfort wrapped in her embrace and realize the words she says is true. The hug ends too soon as she holds me at arms length to take in my appearance once more, her eyes always ending on the moonstone around my neck.

"It seems my magic has not dimmed." She chuckles.

"Did you create this?" I asked, shocked as I instinctively reach for the stone.

"With the help of Elves, yes. Although those Elves have disappeared, their magic lingers, just like it does in the necklace Geminie holds." Shocked at the mention of Elves, I wonder if the Library in the Temple of the Moon Goddess will have any record of them. I know of Lizaria as I have spared with her in Geminie's pack, but i would be nice to see if I can find the original Elves that knew my parents and learn from them after taking back the throne.

"Why are you here, and why haven't we met until now?" I ask Cassandra, wondering where she has been all my life.

"Geminie and Amberle told me they had a theory about you four years ago, about you being the Lost Princess. I wanted to make sure before I met you. Then you moved to Toronto before I could meet you and I decided letting you find who you are on your own was important." She begins to explain, her fingers gently running through my hair as she continues to stare at me.

"When Ira told me you were going to create a pack, I knew that today is the right time for us to meet. It became even better when she told me you would need a barrier in place and I took the chance to build the best barrier possible and made sure the lands became yours the moment you claimed them." The care this Witch has for me causes my tears to spill over, and I am once again pulled into her embrace. First it was Uncle Atti, and now Witch

Cassandra. Who else does Ira know that was around when my parents were alive?

"Cassandra, I think it's time for Crystalline claim this as a new pack. You have years to catch up with the young wolf." Ira cuts in, waiting just behind Cassandra and me. I notice a delicate dagger in her hands, the blade I realise being a sharpened moonstone.

"Since you are claiming land that used to belong to a different pack, you will have to slit your palm open and place it on the doors to the pack house, infusing the blood with the magic of this land." Ira explains as Cassandra pulls away from me and nudges me towards the she-wolf.

[Whose pack was it?] I asked curiously in the private link as I take the dagger and follow Ira up the front steps.

[The one Atticus reported to us two years ago. Amberle and Geminie took in the wolves and then we renovated this place with the intentions of you taking over.] My eyes widen as I look back to Blake and Alice, their demeanor not showing any signs of distress.

[Their old pack?] I ask. Ira nods, confirming my suspicions and I sigh, not knowing if this will bring more harm to the two pups than good.

[Trust me when I say nothing is the same as they remember. And if I am not mistake, they never saw the pack house nor most areas in the pack. The buildings are all new, with the old ones destroyed because of the attack on Nightmare Moon. You can trust me when I say Cassandra cleansed the lands for them and for you.] Taking in Ira's words, I turn the dagger in my hands as I debate weather or not to become Alpha of these lands. It would have been easier had it been absorbed by other packs, but it seems Blake and Alice truly have no bad memories from where we currently stand.

"Blake, Alice... Is this where you want to call home?" I turn, asking the pups. What ever they say will be the answer I accept.

"I don't know why, but I feel at peace here. Is something wrong?" Blake states and I shake my head, happy to know he is fine while we stand here.

"Can I have a big room!" I chuckle at Alice's outburst, realizing that I have nothing to worry about. This will be our home.

"I am pretty sure Albot and Crystalline will give you a big room." Marcie states, giving me a wink. With their approval, I turn back to the door and hold the sharp blade to my hand, slicing it and quickly placing my bleeding palm on the wooden doors.

"I, Princess Crystalline Evangeline Rose Thorn, declare this land and those who come seeking for a family as my own. As Alpha, I will protect and serve my pack to my fullest as well as uphold the law of wolf. This pack will forever be known as Astraea, Greek for starry night." A shimmer spreads from my bloody hand before enveloping the mansion, the magic and power of royal blood coursing out from inside me.

I watch as the shimmering silver light flows down the mansion, enveloping the land. I can see the forest I now own; the large lake I promised Alice we can swim in and the mountains that border the west. The claim to the land ends at the barrier, merging with the magic Cassandra left seamlessly.

Finally, the shimmer ends and the power of Alpha courses through me. But I lost the connection to my rogue pack. With a smile, I stand before my friends, scanning each and every one of them until landing on Albot.

"Albot Everrette, please step forward and accept the role as Beta to Astraea." I call out. I see my friend smiling at me, making quick strides till he towers above me, taking my bleeding palm in his hand gently and swiping his tongue across the bloody cut. I feel our bond snap into place once more, this time stronger as my chosen Beta looks down at me.

From there, I called each wolf to me, accepting Marcie as my Head Tracker, the ex-mercenary having the perfect training to train our future Trackers. Matrix, as requested, became my Head Hunter, the pride in his eyes evident as he ruffles my hair like he always did when we were pups and causing me to growl in annoyance at him.

"Blake, Alice. I never officially adopted you, but will you come and accept me as your mother?" I ask the pups, leaving their initiation for last. Blake looks at me in surprise before rushing into my arms, the sixteen year old already my height and still growing.

"We already consider you our mama." He sniffles, holding back the tears. I smile, wrapping my left arm around him while motioning for Alice to come join the hug. She quickly joins us, my right arm wrapped around her as I hug my pups.

I can feel the bond snap into place, my blood recognizing them as my own. Albot joins us, wrapping his arms around me from behind and I realize in that moment that when the mate bond with Narin breaks, I want Albot to be my mate and father to these two. With a smile, I invite everyone inside allowing everyone to enter the pack house first.

"Mama." Alice calls out, her hand grasping my shirt.

"What is it?" Concerned, I pull her into my arms and smooth her golden hair away from her face.

"I don't like Maya... something is wrong with her aura." She explains. I sigh, placing a kiss on her forehead before taking her hand in mine.

"I know. I don't trust her either."

Chapter 20 – A Hard Conversation

Sunlight filtering through my window and onto my eyes has me waking from the sweet dream I was having. I sigh, closing my eyes for a moment to feel the power humming through my veins.

It's been three months since creating Astraea.

Three months since we started accepting wolves to join.

One day I will have to leave this pack to become Queen, so for now I will take this time in Astraea to practice being a fair and just leader. A groan beside me and a strong arm full of tattoos wrap around my body, drawing me closer to a warm body I feel safe beside. I smile, turning to face Albot who is fast asleep, his face peaceful as he tries to pull me closer.

"Albot, we need to get up." I whisper, poking his cheek. He growls gently, pulling me even closer to him as he buries his face into my hair, inhaling my scent. I smile, relishing in his warmth and waiting for the day we can claim each other as mates. It's something we talked about months after getting to know each other, learning that he too had been rejected by his mate, the daughter of the Alpha to his old pack. After that, he was sold to the Hunters and became a spectacle in the illegal dogfighting ring. He understands the pain I am going through; the feeling of my body being torn apart every time Narin sleeps with another wolf. We bonded over our pain and that bond grew into something more.

Poking his cheek some more, I giggle as he tries to hide from me, pushing his face deeper into the pillow and under my hair, letting out a small growl of warning.

"Crystalline, I am tired." He groans, his voice husky with sleep. His arms tighten around me, holding me close to him and I sigh, trying to figure out how to wake this sleepy wolf. With a smirk, I move my hands to his sides and slowly start to tickle him, gaining a girlish squeal in response as he flings himself backwards landing on the floor with a loud thud.

"Woops." I mumble, sitting on my knees to look over at the startled Albot who glares at me with a glint in his eyes I know all to well.

"One." He growls out in warning. That's all I need to bound off the bed and bolt down the halls of the pack house. Loud footsteps following behind me alerts me to Albot already untangled from the sheets and in pursuit.

"Someone save me!" I laugh, turning a corner just in time to see Marcie and Blake slam open their doors and peek their heads out, ready to fight. Zooming past them, I hear Albot crash into a wall and wince. That must have hurt.

"What did you do!" Marcie calls out laughing.

"She tickled me awake." Albot responds instead as I manage to make it to the stairway. Once I reach outside, I can shift and run into the forest.

"Shit, I need to get a video!" Blake laughs out, already knowing the payback I am going to receive from Albot. Careful not to fall down the stairs as I run, I look behind me to see Albot skidding to a stop just before the decent to smirk at me. Something doesn't feel right.

Next thing I know, he has shifted into his black wolf, using his larger form to bound down the steps and easily catch up to me. With a squeal, I quickly hop over the railing, preparing myself to fall two more floors down and shifting just in time to avoid being injured.

Luckily for me, the large double doors are opened wide as pack mates exit and enter the pack house, giving me a chance to bolt outside just as I hear Albot tumbling down the stairs. I grin, my tongue lolling out as I make a beeline for the trees, my small form becoming nothing but a blur of white in the snow, and I am grateful for the camouflage my white fur brings in winter. I count down each foot step until I can make it to safety away from Albot, already planning to take the treetop highway.

Suddenly, I feel my body being tackled, a wolf pinning me down with their own body. Albot's scent wraps around me as he allows his full weight to crush me while I shiver from the slight cold seeping into my fur, as the wet snow cushions my body.

[Get off you big oaf!] I groan out through our link. I am met with a tongue swiping across my fur before feeling him snuggle closer.

[No, you're comfy.] He chuckles, placing his neck across mine. I sigh, squirming underneath him and trying to get free, only to feel his teeth gently take the scruff of my neck to keep me in place.

[You tickled me awake, so now I keep you trapped.] He states, closing his eyes. I growl, nipping at his paw, trying to annoy him into letting me go. He growls, letting go of my scruff to nip at my ear, and I turn my head, managing to get my teeth onto hit neck, gently gnawing at the skin and pawing at his face.

[You're annoying!] He groans.

[Only with you.] I retort. He sighs, slowly getting to his feet. As he is about to move away from me, a brown wolf tackles him causing the two to roll away in a ball of fur, snarls and growls.

Bolting to my feet, I quickly race to Albot's aid just in time to realize the brown wolf is Matrix. Both wolves are in fight mode, Albot taking the advantage with his years of training in the fighting ring.

With a snarl of my own, I release an Alpha command, causing the two to shiver and back away from one another with Matrix slipping and falling into a snow pile.

[Matrix, explain!] I growl, stalking towards my friend. I watch as he exposes his neck to me, the remorse in his eyes clear as day.

[I thought he was hurting you!] He defends himself, quietly.

[You do realize we are on pack lands right! No wolf can injure me.] Angry at my friend, I make my way to Albot and check his wounds sighing when I realize they are superficial. Nuzzling the man before me, I walk towards Matrix and check his wounds. He may have been the aggressor but Albot definitely wounded Matrix heavily.

[Go to Marcie and get your wounds treated. We start training in three hours.] I order, seeing my friend walk away with a limp, his head hanging low. I will have to talk to him one-on-one soon to settle things.

[You okay?] Albot asks, nuzzling me gently and placing his tail over my body.

[No. Matrix has always been my protector up until two years ago. I think he still believes in protecting me.] I sigh, leaning into the warm body beside me.

[I know how he feels. You look like a pup standing next to me and all I want to do is protect you.]

[What stops you?] I ask, looking up only to find Albot already staring at me.

[The fact that you can easily kick my ass in a fight.] He laughs, swiping his tongue affectionately across my cheek. With wolfish grin, I stretch up to nuzzle his face before trotting towards the house.

[Come on, we have work to do.] I sigh

◆◆◆

"So what do we need to do to grow this pack?" Marcie asks as we all settle into the boardroom. I frown, looking down at my laptop with a list I had made with Geminie and Amberle the first day I created Astraea.

"For one, we need to train our wolves. We only have a small pack of sixty but that doesn't mean we should be skimping on training." I begin, connecting the laptop to the screen behind me so everyone can see the to-do list.

"We should also accept Rogues into our pack. Most Rogues are just looking for a home and running away from their old one." Albot adds and I agree, pulling up a list of names Atticus sent me.

"Lately, Ira and Atticus have been working together to bring down the Hunter's dog fighting rings. This is a list of wolves looking for a pack they can call their own and with Albot being a victim of one he can help settle them in." I suggest, looking around the room to see approval in everyone's expression.

"Some of these wolves look like they will make great Hunters." Matrix chimes in, his eyes filled with excitement at training new wolves.

"Don't forget we also need teachers and doctors in the pack." I remind him, getting a dismissive wave.

"We have a hospital and a school just outside the border." He retorts with and I frown.

"It's a human hospital. Atticus and I have been in contact with a few packs in the area to create a small tourist town by the large lake in unclaimed territory and make it a neutral place for all." I begin, bringing up a large piece of land situated by a lake. With the birds-eye-view on display, I begin talking about the plan to open local businesses for packs to work in, a bed and breakfast by the lake for travelers both human and supernatural to enjoy, with a school to be built and a hospital on the other side of the plans.

"This could work." Marcie smiles excited, asking for control of the mouse as she maps out a town square and parks for children to play in.

"We would have a safe place for pups to learn that will be included in the Ontario Government database while also bringing in revenue to the town." I turn to see Matrix looking at the plans with interest, his nonchalance gone as he observes the town layout.

"We would need a police force there." He mumbles and I chuckle.

"Yes, we will. There will be a meeting with the three Alphas close by next month to discuss everything and I intend to bring all of you." With everyone on board, I move to the next topic, creating a training schedule.

"We can do what Blood Moon and Silver Crystal Crescent does, train the Hunters and Trackers together and have set days and times depending on age." Matrix suggests, pride swelling inside me at my best friend.

"That means you and I will have to come up with a training regimen." Marcie sighs.

"You two can have a week to figure it out and bring the proposal to me next Monday." With a chuckle, I give the two time to talk, deciding that having Marcie as my Head Tracker and Matrix as my Head Hunter was a great idea three months ago.

"Now we should probably talk about Crystalline taking back her throne." Cassandra chimes in. The witch has become a resident here, having a small cottage close to the lake where she can pray to Morai and guide Alice and me.

The last three months with this witch by my side, telling me stories of my parents and sister as well as how Coro was trained before being banished has been great help in my training. She helped me to learn how to combat dark spells and how to protect my pack from hexes using moonflowers blessed under the full moon.

"Atticus has a few ideas he will be sharing when him and Heidi come for Christmas next week." I explain, turning to look out the window. A light snow fall has begun and I smile, thinking about my first Christmas in Toronto. It was a mild snowfall back then, the city becoming quiet and cozy while Blake, Alice, Albot and I walked the streets to see the lights at the

Christmas market. Maybe we should decorate the pack house, with this year being the first official Christmas in Astraea.

"Well then, I guess for now we work on growing the pack and training. I can see if Alexander will want to meet the new pack and Alpha. We can say Albot is the new Alpha looking to make an alliance." Cassandra states, bringing my attention to her. Mulling over her words, I write this suggestion on my to do list before adjourning the meeting.

"Trix, can you stay back for a moment?" I ask as everyone begins to file out. Confused, my friend walks forward, taking the seat beside me that was vacated by Albot as we wait for the room to clear.

"What's up, Crysta?" He asks.

"It's about earlier when you attacked Albot." I see the shame in his eyes instantly as his head droops. His fingers begin to fidget and I sigh, reaching out and clasping his hands.

"Trix, we aren't the same wolves we were two years ago. We have been training and gaining experience outside the Royal Pack and becoming stronger." With soft words, I try to show Matrix I am not mad but that this talk is necessary for the both of us.

"I know, Crysta, but every time I look at you, I see the wolf I trained and protected my whole life. I see the girl I grew up with, my best friend. But more importantly, I see the woman I fell for and wanted." His eyes stares into my own, his confession shocking me as our fingers intertwine. To think we both fell for each other as we grew up. It was always us against the world, Matrix and I always having each other's back while we trained and studied, even if he is two years older than me.

"Trix—"

"Crystalline, I watched you turn eighteen and be rejected, watched as you crumbled in pain. If it weren't for the fact you needed me, I would have killed Narin that day. It took everything in me to watch you leave for Toronto and not follow you. And now you come back with Albot. I can see the way you two look at each other and I hate it. Hate knowing he was by your side for two years protecting you—"

"Albot doesn't protect me." I cut him off. Sighing, I release our hands and lean back into my chair, running fingers through my hair as I look out the window.

"He treats me as an equal, as a strong she wolf despite my size. I am one of few wolves that can best him and because of that he respects me." I continue, a small smile growing on my face as I think about the tattooed silent wolf that always stood beside me, never behind nor in front.

"You always stood in front of me, never giving me a chance to grow. I need you to now stand behind me, to let me grow and become a strong Queen." Turning back, I try to ignore the hurt in Matrix's eyes as I take a deep breath.

"I know my words hurt, but we can't continue the way we have. I can't hide behind my pack - my family - for protection." I continue, knowing that my words will sting Matrix even more.

"You love him, don't you." It's a statement, not a question.

"I do, Trix. You will always be my best friend. The wolf that protected me when I needed it. What we have is gone now because we are not the same as we once were." I confirm, wanting to reassure my friend.

"But." This one word is whispered and my heart breaks, seeing the pain in his eyes.

"But with Albot, he treats me as his equal. He respects me as a powerful wolf and accepts me for who I am." I can see him mulling over my words before he closes his eyes and stands, walking towards the door. He pauses halfway reaching for the handle before turning to look at me with sad eyes.

"Thank you for talking to me, Crysta. If you don't mind, I need some time alone."

"Take your time, Trix. I'll always be your friend." With that, I watch him walk out the door before I allow the tears to fall. This conversation hurt more than I thought it would, and a distance between me and Matrix grew. I just hope I don't lose my best friend.

Strong arms lift me from my chair and I instinctively wrap mine around the owner, taking in Albot's scent. "It's just us, Crystalline. You can cry." He whispers soothingly, and cry I do.

Chapter 21 – A Hidden Spy

Staring at the photos on my desk sent by Atticus, I sigh. It seems my hunch was right with not trusting her. Suddenly, the door to my office is thrown open and a frazzled looking Matrix walks in, his hair in disarray and his clothing crumpled. I haven't seen him since last week when Maya and he got into a fight.

"Crysta, I need your help." He starts, closing the door before pacing the length of the room. Putting the photos into the folder, I wait for Matrix to settle down and explain, even though I would like to yell at him for entering without knocking. He knows the rule of not barging into my office. I listen to him muttering to himself, running his fingers through his hair before plopping onto the chair in front of my desk with a pained groan.

"It's Maya. She has been demanding I mark her for over a year, but I can't. Something feels wrong when I am with her." He complains. Studying his face, I see just how haggard my friend has become since last week, his eyes holding an array of emotions. With a small smile, I grab a water bottle from my mini fridge and walk around to sit beside him.

"Matrix, take a deep breath." Placing a hand gently on his shoulder, I try my best to calm his frazzled nerves.

"I need you to start from the beginning." With a sigh, Matrix takes the offered drink and chugs it in one go and place the empty bottle onto the desk.

"For the last year since meeting Maya, our relationship never felt right. I have tried multiple times to mark her, to claim her as mine, but something inside me stops me from doing anything." Running his fingers through his hair again, Matrix stands and begins pacing the length of my office.

"It feels forced, like we aren't meant to be, but I can't deny the mate pull even if it is faint." He stops, looking out the window with a pained growl. I want to rush to him, to give my friend a hug, but doing so may make him feel worse.

"And then I started training with Marcie and it just feels so right with her." He continues, turning to lean against the glass and look at me with pained filled eyes.

"Help me make sense of this, please?" With a sigh, I motion for Matrix to sit again, reaching for the folder on my desk. He watches me, most likely debating on if he wants to hear what I have to say, before returning to the chair he vacated.

"Before I share what I have learned, do you think Maya is your true mate?" I ask him. I need to know if he genuinely believe Maya and him are meant to be, or if there is a chance she is playing him.

"I don't." He sighs. His shoulders slump in defeat and the taste of heartbreak lingers in the air.

"Then I think you should know she is a spy for Alexander. Atticus with the help of Heidi had a Rogue pretend to be a liaison for the network Coro has. Maya has been keeping tabs on me and sending information to Coro. Some we let slip through, others we take and tweak the information." I begin, taking out the photographs one by one and handing them to Matrix. I can see the fury in his eyes, the pain and hatred for a she-wolf he thought was his mate.

"Why didn't you tell me before?" I wince as he directs his anger to me, watching as he throws the pictures onto the desk and start pacing once more.

"I wanted to, but I had no idea how you would react or if you would believe me. I needed to wait, for the good of the pack." Taking a deep breath, I pull out one last picture and wait for Matrix to pace past me before handing him the final picture.

"I believe this witch is the reason why you think she is your mate." I state, sighing as I hand him the picture of Maya meeting with a witch, one I learned is a descendant of Avilla.

"Why would a witch be involved?!" His fingers grip the paper, clutching it so hard that he nearly tears the edges.

"Because this witch specializes in dark charms. Do you know if Maya wears a piece of jewelry, one that she never takes off?" My words have his pacing faltering, his brows furrowed as he thinks. Waiting patiently, I get up and take out a moonstone ring from a safe with the stone set in silver. With a smile, I carefully walk towards Matrix who's eyes snap to mine.

"There is this ring... It's solid gold with rubies in it." I nod, taking his right hand and sliding the ring onto his middle finger, the smell of moonflowers filling the air.

"I have a feeling that's a charm, like this one. Cassandra taught me how to harness my powers that I inherited from my mother to make these. What I need you to do is kiss near the ring. If it smells sweet like candy or rancid like decay, then that is why you believe she is your mate." I explain, relief settling inside me as my fingers circle the stone in the ring.

"How do I do that?" His voice is a whisper, his fingers lacing through mine before his free hand pulls me in for a hug, holding me tight and taking in my scent.

"You go to her room and pretend to make up. The charm I give you will keep your mind clear enough to distinguish the charm." We stand in silence after this, Matrix taking his time to calm himself.

Since our conversation nine months ago, our friendship has been rocky. Some days we end up fighting, other days it's like nothing ever changed between us

Hopefully after today, things will get better and Matrix can find his true mate.

•••

Sitting on the porch, I watch Alice running around with the pups her age, enjoying the simplicity of my pup after a hard morning. Matrix asked if he could take a few hours to settle before confronting Maya, and I agreed. If he were to confront her now with the news of her being a spy and using him still fresh in his mind, it could lead to the she-wolf bolting away.

"I have some news." Albot says from behind me, causing me to groan. What situation do I have to deal with now.

"That reaction tells me you've had a bad day." He comes to sit beside me, pulling me into his lap. I smile, leaning into his touch and allowing my stress to melt away while his left hand gently combs through my hair.

"More like a bad morning. The day isn't over yet." With a sigh, I turn my face into his chest, taking in his scent as we sit in silence for a moment. I just need to be held, even if it is just for a few minutes.

"Hopefully my news is good, then. Alexander wants to meet the Alpha of Astraea." Bolting up right, my eyes scan his face and concluding that what he says is true. It is rare for Alexander to want to meet a new Alpha, believing that strength comes from established packs with hundreds of years already put into them. A new pack is nothing to him until they pass the one-hundred year mark of being established.

"How?" I ask in disbelief.

"A few of our allies don't want to be allied to him and want the true ruler on the throne. They put in a good word for us saying I am the Alpha. The rumor of you being the Lost Princess has spread through the online forums thanks to Ira, Gem and Ams, and many want to see you succeed in getting rid of him." Albot explains, a wide grin on his face. My own grin spreads across my face as I fling my arms around his shoulders, kissing his cheek in happiness.

He did it.

He found a way for us to sneak into the Royal pack and take back what is rightfully mine.

"I'll take that I did an amazing job?" He asks with a smirk, his fingers pinching my chin gently as he looks into my eyes.

"You did an amazing job!"

"Good. He wants us to be there on the next full moon. He plans to sign a treaty with us at a masquerade ball." A frown replaces my smile with this new information. The next full moon is in three weeks. Meaning we have three weeks to weed Maya out as a traitor and three weeks to prepare our pack for my leaving. If things go well, I will be crowned Queen. If things go wrong, I will be dead.

Chapter 22 – Weeding out a Spy

"You excited to return up north?" Marcie asks as I check off what I would need for this trip on my list. I grimace, thinking about how I was treated growing up and look my friend in the eye.

"Honestly, no. That place was a nightmare. But if me taking the throne means bettering werewolf kind, then I will do it." Marcie gives me a small smile before pulling me in for a hug, her comfort being something I need in this moment. We have a week to head up north, a week to see Alexander and Narin.

My heart clenches at the mention of my ex-mate, the reminder that the bond has not yet broken when last night Albot had to hold me once more through the pain of Narin fucking some she-wolf.

At one point, I thought about getting back at him, at allowing Narin to feel the pain I felt by giving in and allow Albot to swallow me in his touch.

But I want my first time to be special.

"I wish I can come with you; help take out that bastard and beat the crap out of that ex-mate of yours." The Latina sighs out, causing me to laugh. To think one of he stupidest things Alexander did was send this spitfire of a she-wolf my way and allowing me to gain a trusted friend.

"Trust me, I need you to take care of Astraea. Besides, you'll be there to help me kill off Coro." I reassure her, the two of us deciding that I can finish packing tonight and that a break is much needed. We walk down the steps of the pack house, intending on going to the kitchen and see what is for lunch, when a flustered Matrix comes running through the door with panic in his eyes.

Grabbing Marcie and I by the hand, he drags us to a quiet sitting room without warning and I link Albot to come join us. Something tells me this panic has to do with Maya.

"Matrix, calm down." Marcie growls, ripping her wrist from his grip and glaring at the panicked wolf. I sigh, pulling my hand free from his grasp as well and taking a seat in an arm chair while I wait for Albot, who thankfully arrives minutes later with a look of concern on his face.

"I left Blake in charge of training the pups. What's so urgent?" He asks, closing the door and leaning against the wooden object to prevent anyone from entering the room.

"Crysta was right. Maya has a charm on her. I finally got the courage to confront her, to make up." Matrix begins, his pacing becoming faster. I look to Albot and frown. We knew she was a spy and thankfully we prevented any damaged this she-wolf could have caused after meeting her.

"Last night I talked to her, talked about having a mating ceremony on next month just to get her to warm up to me and I managed to kiss the hand with that ring she never takes off. I swear, the rancid smell and taste I got nearly made me throw up. I couldn't believe just how horrible it was." He runs his fingers through his hair, his eyes a little sunken in as if he hasn't slept a wink in the last twenty-four hours.

[Blake, I need you to take the pups ages fifteen and under to the training hall. No one is allowed out until I say so.] I link my son.

[Something happened?] the seventeen year old asks.

[Yes. I don't want the pups involved.] With that, I open the link to the pack, making sure my emotions are calmed as to not cause suspicion.

[There will be a pack meeting in thirty minutes outside of the pack house. All pups ages fifteen and under must report to the training hall. All wolves sixteen and older must attend the meeting.] I get a resounding "Yes, Alpha." Before anyone can ask questions, I shut off my link. Right now, I need to focus on Matrix and calming him down.

"So, we are getting rid of a spy." Marcie asks, a predatorial glint in her eyes.

"Yes." I answer with a smirk. I have wanted to tear into that she-wolf for a year now, only being able to spar with her in training and rough her up enough to leave her bedridden for a few days.

Today is the day I make an example of what happens when you mess with my pack.

Climbing out of my chair, I walk towards the still pacing Matrix and force him to stop, having my friend look me in the eye.

"Trix, you need to calm down. I want you to link Maya and tell her you told me about your plan to have a mating ceremony. Make her feel like this meeting is about that." I order, knowing that without an Alpha command, his emotions will be felt through their link. I watch as he takes a deep breath, his eyes glazing over. I wait, allowing him to do what he has to do to make Maya feel like she has won. Finally, his gaze snaps back to mine and he nods.

"She will be there." He confirms.

"Good. We have twenty minutes until the meeting, go take a quick shower and get something to eat." With that, Albot opens the door to allow Matrix upstairs. Hopefully he can hold his emotions together for the time being and we can deal with the Spy quickly.

◆◆◆

Standing on the steps to the pack house, I watch as pack members slowly trickle in. Thankfully, there are no wolves under the age of sixteen in the mix. We didn't need someone helpless for Maya to use as a hostage. We had a few link Albot saying they could not end the patrol and risk Soulless sneaking in. All Albot said was if they see Maya before the meeting ends, to bring her to the pack house.

"Everyone is here." Albot whispers into my ear as I scan the wolves gathered and spot Maya right in front. Good, this will make exposing her easy.

Taking a deep break, I look beside me to make sure Albot, Marcie and Matrix are standing by my side. I will need Matrix to play along as a soon to be fully mated wolf if this plan is to succeed.

"Pack members, I would like to thank you all for gathering here." I begin, taking a step forward and smiling at the crowd. I see the questioning gazes all looking in my direction. The whispers and speculations of why they were gathered with little notice so quickly.

"Now, we have some news about a pack member and I would like to share it. Maya, will you come stand beside me?" Shocked looks are throne Maya's way, the she-wolf beaming with happiness. I watch as she bounds up the stairs, her eyes instantly looking towards Matrix just behind us. I can see the anger in his eyes and inwardly groan. I cannot have him blowing it. Taking Maya's right hand in mine, I feel the ring subtly and suppress a wince. I can feel the dark magic seeping out. Definitely a Dark Witch is involved.

"Now, as you all may know, Maya is the mate to our Head Hunter Matrix. They have yet to have a mating ceremony, and there is a reason why." My smile soon falls as my hand slides up her wrist. Marcie and Albot step forwards, grabbing Maya on either side. I watch the panic form on her face, the fear as my claws did into the wrist. She struggles to get loose, but the two do not relent and I chuckle.

"You all know that Astraea has an opportunity to become allies to the Royal Pack, and that's not false information. Unfortunately, it will not be with Alexander." I begin, stopping to motion for the wolf with his hand in the air.

"Why is that Alpha?" Pedro asks, worry on his face.

"Why don't I let Maya explain. She is a spy, after all." I chuckle out darkly, my claws sinking further into her flesh. Murmurs of disbelief is heard over the crowd while Maya continues to struggle and I sigh.

"Maya, tell these people why you are here." Thankfully, she is still a pack member, my command still holding power over the she-wolf as her struggling stops and the panic in her eyes grows.

"Because you are Princess Crystalline Thorn, and my Master, Prince Coro, ordered me to spy on you for King Alexander." She blurts out, unable to defy my Alpha Command. Growls of the betrayal from the pack are directed at Maya, their hatred towards her growing.

"Why are you mad at me, she lied about being the Lost Princess!" Maya screams out accusingly at the crowd. I chuckle, taking a glace at the she-wolf before digging my claws further into her wrist, feeling her wince. She does not cry out in pain, which doesn't surprise me, she is Coro's underling.

"I never hid who I am. If they came and asked me, I told them the truth. I will never hide anything from my pack." I sneer at her, relishing the defeated look on her face as she realizes this is a trap. The she perks up, a smile of triumph as she smirks at me.

"But I am Matrix's mate!"

"Want to bet on that as a fact?" I ask, my free hand reaching for her ring. Her triumphant look crumbles as I slowly tug the gold ring off of her hand, releasing my claws from her wrist when she tries to resist and prying the ring finger open, breaking it in the process.

Finally, the ring is off and I toss the jewelry into a bowl of Moon Water. The surface begins to bubble, a black tar like liquid seeping to the surface. The crowd backs away, terrified of the black magic being released and purified.

"Matrix, do you feel the mate bond?" I ask, my eyes never leaving Maya's face in case the she-wolf tries anything. Silence follows my question as I wait for his answer, but it never comes.

"Matrix?" I call out again.

"Um... Alpha, you should take a look." Someone in the crowd calls out with a chuckle. Looking away from Maya, I turn to see Marcie loosening her grip on the she-wolf as Matrix makes his way to her. It's as if no one else but those two are on the porch. Like their worlds only involve the two of them.

"Clearly he feels a mate bond, but it's not with Maya." Albot chuckles, taking Maya's other arm just as Marcie lets go and rushes to Matrix, wrapping herself in his embrace as he buries his face into her hair, inhaling her scent.

"Hey, M and M, can we finish with this traitor first before you go off to mate?" I call out laughing, watching as Marcie and Matrix jump away from each other, a blush on their faces.

"S-sorry, Crystalline..." Marcie mumbles breathlessly, causing me to laugh again. I wave a hand dismissively at them, deciding not to give the two a hard time, considering they have spent a year unable to be with each other because of Maya and her dark charm.

"So, with Maya being proven as a traitor who used a dark charm on Matrix, the punishment is simple. She will be banished from the pack and turned Rogue." I begin, taking a moment to see the anger on the crowds face growing.

"That's it?!"

"Yeah, that's a shitty punishment!"

"She should be beaten!"

"She should be killed!"

The crowd protests and I allow them to voice their frustrations, happy to know they too feel hurt by this betrayal.

"This is not it at all. If you remember I have all the pups kept to the training room it is because I do not want any of them to witness what is to happen." Talking above the crowd and quieting them, I put the power in my blood into each word. Happy when their attention if focused onto me, I turn to Maya with a grin.

"Maya Alibass, you are hence forth banished from Astraea. You will be marked a traitor and upon Albot releasing you, have exactly two hours from leaving my pack lands. Be warned though. You are only allowed a ten-minute head start before my pack hunts you down, allowed to kill you as a Rogue and traitor." With that, I motion for Albot to follow me, dragging Maya as we walk towards the crowd, intending to pass by them and allow Maya a clear head start.

The wolves before us part, giving us a pathway while they curse the now Rogue she-wolf who whimpers in pain from the mark of a traitor burning into her arm from the power of my words. With the crowd behind us, I nod to Albot who promptly releases her. Maya stumbles forward, turning to glare at me. I growl, something feral and powerful giving her a warning.

She can either fight me and die or run and have a chance to live.

She chooses to run, turning around and heading into the trees. It takes about two hours to reach the border in wolf form. Although in just a few minutes she will be hunted by my pack. A pack filled with wolves who came looking for a second chance after facing a betrayal do not take kindly to traitors. Maya will be dead in no time.

"You can hunt." My words are a trigger as the wolves behind me surge forward, some shifting into their fur side while others take the challenge in their human form. I chuckle, looking around the now empty front lawn to see Marcie and Matrix leaning against the railing on the porch, making out like hormonal pups.

"Not going to join the hunt?" I ask, amused when the two separate with a look of shock and embarrassment.

"She isn't worth it." Matrix mumbles, his eyes never leaving Marcie. I chuckle, linking my arm through Albot's and heading towards the pack house.

"How about you two head back to Matrix's place and finish mating, then. She wasted a year of your time with one another." I suggest, seeing the two nodding approvingly at this before Matrix scoops Marcie into his arms and runs off. I will be surprised if a pup isn't born next year because of this.

"What are we going to do?" Albot asks, nuzzling my cheek with his lips. I shiver, looking at him with a pointed look before dragging him inside.

"We are going to raid the kitchen, find food and hide away in bed for the rest of the day. Link the pack to pick up their pups when they finish hunting." My answer is met with a chuckle from him, his lips pressing a soft kiss on my cheek before his eyes glaze over. I know that me not accepting his advances hurt him, but the mate bond still hums weakly in my veins. I want it to be gone before I can enjoy anything with Albot.

Chapter 23 - Farewell, Astraea

Filling my travel mug with coffee, I groan at the magic bean juice waking me up. Albot woke those who are traveling north to the Royal Pack at four in the morning, wanting everyone fully ready to leave by five thirty.

We plan to bring thirty wolves out of the two hundred that joined Astraea, these wolves already devoting their loyalty to me as the Princess and not as their Alpha. They know the risk, having been training with Matrix in the ways of the Royal Pack Warriors and know that any moment, they could possibly lose their lives.

"You okay, sunshine?" Marcie asks, her tired yet happy eyes running up and down my body.

"I. Want. Sleep." With a groan between each word, I walk into her open arms and allow my friend to hug me. She will be here, taking care of Astraea while we are gone, and having the wolves train in case of any retaliation from Coro.

"I know, hun. Albot said he will drive your Hummer so you can get your beauty sleep." She teases with a chuckle, pulling on my simple braid. I growl lightly, earning another chuckle from Marcie as she pulls away to look me in the eye.

"You got this, Crystalline. You go there, kill Alexander at that ball, and take the throne. Then we kill that brother of yours and work on eradicating the Soulless." Her words are encouraging as we both smile at each other. If things go the way we want them to, I will be Queen and Marcie will be the Luna of Astraea.

"Crystalline, you ready to go?" Albot steps into the room, leaning against the door frame as his smiling face finds mine. Marcie nudges me, a smirk on her own tanned face and I glare at her, already knowing the hidden meaning. She cannot wait for the day my mate bond breaks and I can be with Albot.

"Yes, are Alice and Blake in the Hummer already?" I ask with a yawn, Albot pushing himself off the door frame as I walk towards him, taking his outstretched hand.

"Yes. Blake wants to drive if that's fine. This just means you can use me as a pillow and sleep longer." He answers. I smile, happy that my pup can drive now without much trouble and agreeing that Blake could use more practice. He will be leaving for college next year in Toronto and interning with Atticus in the fall.

Marcie walks with us to the front door, the pack already waiting to go as we all say our final goodbyes to everyone. Matrix comes to me, pulling me away from Albot and into a hug.

"Thank you, Crysta, and be safe." He whispers. I close my eyes, taking in my best friend's scent before releasing him and watching him take his place next to Marcie. They will be great leaders of Astraea, and I cannot wait to watch them continue to grow this pack.

"I will call you when we reach the Royal Pack." I assure him, seeing the pained look in his eyes. It kills him knowing he can't be there by my side, but Marcie and him are needed here to protect the pack from Alexander and Coro's allies. They are also needed to help those in need of a second chance find a new home. The sad thing is, I realize that I no longer need the two wolves as my protectors.

With one last goodbye, I climb into the back seat of my Hummer, Alice and Blake already settled in with the GPS ready to go.

"This was the land Nightmare Moon sat on, wasn't it?" Alice states quietly, shocking me.

"Yes... How did you find out?" I asked confused as Blake lets out a sigh.

"We knew the day we arrived here. We just didn't want to say anything because the truth is, we were happy to be able to see our parents' graves again. Besides, Nightmare Moon no longer exists and to know this place gained a second chance because of you, made us even happier." Blake explains, turning in his seat to smile at me. Tears well in my eyes at the trust the pups put into me. They had faith in me to keep them safe and happy.

"Well, Marcie and Trix already said you are welcome back anytime." I sniffle, wiping away a stray tear.

"Yeah, but you're our mom now. Our home is with you." With that, Blake turns back to face the front, turning the Hummer on and driving away. Hopefully, this last move will be their forever home and we can all live peacefully together once more.

Chapter 24 – Royal Pack

"So this is the Royal Pack lands." Alice asks, her eyes scanning the border as we approach a patrol. Albot had called ahead an hour ago, letting the liaison of the pack know our estimated arrival. Now, we just wait for the guards to do their inspections before gaining the okay to enter their lands

"We still have two hours to go before we reach the palace." I inform her, doing my best to stay quiet and inconspicuous as we pass by many houses and the small town.

"Do you think the charm Cassandra gave you will work?" Albot sighs with worry, his eyes never leaving the Royal Guards as they search through the many vehicles we brought, their watchful eyes making sure there is no threat to Alexander. I stay silent, a guard coming towards my Hummer with a worried look on their face. Albot rolls down the window, his features a mask of calm as he greets the wolf in front of him politely.

"Alpha Albot, it looks like someone had silver on them, could you explain yourself?" The guard asks. Silently cursing, I open the link.

[Who is the idiot that brought silver?] I demand, putting an Alpha command into my words.

[My mate packed it for me for self defence. It's a dagger with the edge coated in silver. I am so sorry; I had no clue.] I sigh as a Hunter named Daniel answers, realizing he left a pregnant mate back at Astraea with the promise to return safe and alive. No wonder there was a weapon in his suitcase. Albot relays the message to the guard, explaining it was a gift from that wolf's pregnant mate and meant no harm. I smile with how smoothly he can lie, making it seem like an innocent accident.

"So his mate packed it for him?" The guard asks.

"Yes. I mean, my own mate is in the back with our pup so I know how he feels. The last mission I went on, she gave me a vial of wolfsbane to throw at an enemy if need be." The men chuckles at Albot's words and I roll my eyes.

Thankfully, the guards believe us and within moments we cross the border. I shiver as the familiar magic rushes over me, goosebumps forming on my skin.

Hopefully, Alexander isn't alerted to a wolf with Royal Blood entering the territory. Knowing him, he is probably too preoccupied by a pack whore to even care. Soon, he will be dead.

I settle into my seat, relieved to know the first part of our plan has succeeded—entering the Royal Pack unnoticed. Tonight is the masquerade ball. As such, we will not be meeting with Alexander until it is time to forge an Alliance. Little does he know the moment he steps onto the stage I will be there waiting to rip his throat out.

I will kill him and then kill my brother. Reminding my pack to be on their best behaviour until it's time, I close the link and choose to take a nap. Alice and Blake will be fine as long as we stay in the car, and it turns out the charm I am wearing will keep my scent hidden from the Royal Pack. My only concern is what will happen if I run into my mate.

Will the charm work, or will he instantly recognize me?

◆◆◆

Growling as I try to tie the bodice of my ballgown, I let out a frustrated sigh. I already miss the days where I didn't have to worry about ballgowns and sequins, heels and accessories. Thankfully, I have my silver dagger ready to be strapped to my thigh the moment I can get this infuriating blue ballgown on.

"Crystalline?" I knock on my door and Albot's voice gives me some hope as I see him walk inside the room, an amused smile on his face as he takes in my dishevelled look.

"Need a hand?" He chuckles, taking quick strides and gently turns me to face the mirror as his nimble fingers make quick work of the corset straps. I smile, watching the reflection in the mirror and thank who ever was watching over us the day I rescued Albot.

"There, all done." His arms snake around my waist, pulling me into his body where his deep brown eyes stare into mine in the mirror, his black hair styled on top of his head contrasting my curly white hair.

"Crystalline, I—"

"Albot, when the mate bond breaks between me and Narin, I want to be mated to you." I blurt out, leaning my head against his shoulder and smiling at his surprised look.

"When will it break, Crystalline?" He asks, a whimper in his voice as his lips kiss the nape of my neck. I shiver, mulling over his question before turning to face him, cupping his cheeks in my hands and smiling gently at the man before me.

"Tonight. Either it breaks willingly or I break it by killing him. It all depends on how loyal Narin is to Alexander." I see the look of shock he has to my statement. No wolf has ever willingly killed their mate, but I don't care. Narin is the wolf I rejected, the wolf I did not want in my life. If the Deity above did not break our bond the moment I kill Alexander, then I will do it for them.

I want Albot, I want the love and respect he has for me, the partnership we have grown since the first night I saved him. I do not want any other wolf but him and the only thing standing in our way is the stupid mate bond.

"You sure about this?" Albot asks, worry in his eyes at the potential killing of my rejected mate.

"Positive. Not only did he reject me for being a runt, but he is Alexander's current Beta. I refuse to keep those loyal to him and Coro alive. They will only bring destruction to our kind." My answer seems to settle his worry, as Albot leans forward, his lips consuming mine in a gentle kiss. The world seems to fade away in this short brief moment before we need to leave, and I relish the feeling of love and adoration radiating off of Albot.

But the kiss is cut short as the clock chimes the hour. We only have an hour left before the ball and everyone needs to be ready.

Three quick knocks followed by one long one tells me my pack mates are ready and I link them to come in and to be careful not to be seen. The she-wolves already have their makeup and hair done, a mask on their face. They frown when they see me, hair still a mess and face still clean.

"Alpha, on the chair, we need to prepare you." A she-wolf, Lilac, mock orders, three other she-wolves following her to where I stand as they usher me into the vanity chair. I look to Albot for help, but he just backs away, hands up in surrender as he joins the others, an amused look on everyone's face.

"I need to talk about the plan!" I protest, getting a pointed look from the brunet Heather before she grabs a brush and starts to deal with my hair.

[I have a feeling I won't be able to talk while these ladies do their work so let's get this meeting going.] I send out through the link, making sure that all thirty wolves that joined me on this mission are in.

Only fifteen chosen wolves will be at the ball, the other fifteen already geared and waiting to fight with Blake and Alice hiding in Albot's room. I will not allow anyone to harm my pups.

[The alliance ceremony will not take place until midnight, which is three hours away. This means we have an hour to finish preparing to fight.] I begin, motioning for Albot to continue when Lilac pulls on my chin and forces me to turn my face in her direction as she begins my makeup.

[We already have a list of who is truly devoted to Alexander thanks to Atticus and his spies. This means while we are mingling with the crowd at the ball, the rest of you in your rooms will be sneaking through the halls, finding those loyal to Alexander and Coro, and eliminating them.] Albot continues, his eyes never looking away as the women basically torture me.

[Understood, Beta. What do we do if we come across pups?] Someone asks and I sigh.

[Use the sleep powder Cassandra gave us. If they are with their parents, use it on all of them and tie the parents up. We can have Cassandra and her coven dream walk them to see where their loyalties lie. We do not kill the innocents.] I answer. This results in a *Yes, Alpha* through the link and I smile, only to be scolded by Heather for ruining my lipstick and having some of my makeup wiped away.

I decide to sit still, allowing the girls to finish their work while Albot reminds everyone to be casual and friendly towards the others attending today, to not put their drinks down and if they do, immediately get a new drink in case someone tries to drug them. We cannot be too careful when it comes to our safety.

[Has anyone realized Crystalline is with us?] Harry asks, his blue eyes directed at me.

[Thankfully, no. My only concern is my ex-mate, Narin. The bond hasn't broken yet so not only are you mingling with guests, but your job is also to keep Narin away from me before we can enact our plan.] Is my response,

Harry giving me a nod of understanding. With fifteen minutes to spare, my makeup and hair is complete and the ladies spin the chair to allow me a chance to see their work.

I gasp in shock, the light makeup using peach and blue tones around my eyes making the prismatic colour pop. My hair is carefully curled, left to cascade down my back with a small white gold clip used to keep some from falling into my face.

Finally, Albot walks towards me with a simple wooden box in hand, a sly smile on his face.

"Atticus told me this is for you." He says softly, opening the box to reveal a delicately crafted mask. The mask is shaped like a crescent moon, the lower portion will be covering my eyes while the upper portion will be slightly above my hair line.

What surprises me the most is that it is made with silver threads with a small delicate chain holding a pearl-sized moonstone falling from the tip of the top peak. A mask only I can wear, a piece of silver that could be used as a weapon, and a moonstone that I have a feeling Cassandra enchanted with another charm to keep my identity a secret.

With a smile, I gently place the delicate mask onto my face and fasten the straps at the back. Taking the offered hand Albot holds out to me, I stand and allow Lilac to carefully hand my dagger to me, slipping it through the hidden pocket of my gown and securing it into the thigh holster for it. Satisfied with our plan, I turn to look at my pack mates - the wolves I gave a second chance too and who whole heartedly support me - and take a deep breath. Tonight will change our lives either for the best or for worst depending on if this mission succeeds.

"Lets not keep Alexander waiting, this will be a ball to die for."

Chapter 25 – Royal Ball

Once again, I find myself standing before the grand doorway to the ballroom, my pack being one of the earlier guests to arrive. I swallow nervously, the memories of that happened last time I stood here flooding through my mind like a movie set to fast forward. I feel dizzy, worried with a slight unease settling in my stomach. With so many wolves around, I realize in this moment that we have only one option and that is to kill Alexander or die trying.

My pack is already mingling with those who came to witness a new pack make an alliance with their King, their curious gazes on Albot and I as I cling to his arm and try my best to steady my frantically beating heart. Thankfully, no one has recognized me but that can change drastically if Narin ever gets close to me.

[You okay Crystalline?] Albot asks, his eyes searching mine.

[No but I will be.] I admit, snuggling closer to his side and eyeing all the wolves around us. All are chatting away nonchalantly, asking about their pack and how they have been combatting Rogues and Soulless. It sickens me to hear how one wolf had his pack capture the Rogues that trespassed onto his lands and allowed his Hunters to hunt them down and rip them apart. His pack will be first to go when I claim the throne.

"Ladies and gentlemen." A voice calls out over the crowd. I smile, realizing that Butler Loki is still alive. At least I will have one ally tonight inside the Royal Pack. When every one settles, their attention on the butler, he continues with a smile.

"The ball is going to begin. Please enjoy the night before a new alliance is made." With this the doors are opened by the guards. Wolves quickly make their way into the grand ballroom while I stand back with Albot, not wanting to see the place where my life changed just yet. With majority of the guests inside, I am coaxed into walking through the double doors by Albot and my pack mates, telling me to not let fear win as I will be Queen by the end of the night and I need to claim this room, this Palace as my own.

Of course, they are right and with a deep breath I stand straighter, shoulders back and head held high. I am the true heir and no one has the right to intimidate me.

Walking into the ballroom, the first thing I notice is the dais, the one directly in the moon's path where Geminie and I once stood. Where Narin rejected me and where the journey of the last three years began. With a small smile, I lead Albot down the stairs towards the dancefloor, where a waltz is taking place to the music played by the band in the corner. To say I am surprised that they are wolves and not humans is an understatement, but at least this way no humans will become casualties when the fighting begins. Albot smiles, his eyes on me as he twirls me around the dance floor in time to the music.

[How is the hunt going?] I ask through the link. I see Albot chuckle while various of my pack mates who have found dance partners try to hide their smirk. The operation has started.

[We already have two found and killed. No pups just yet.] Stan calls out through the link, a hint of amusement in their voice. I chuckle, closing my eyes to keep me linking my pack unnoticed from those around us.

[Make that three!] Lisa chuckles. Proud of the work my pack is doing, I remind them to stay safe and the rules of protect pups who are innocent in all of this before closing the link. Now it is out turn. We have an hour to kill before Alexander arrives which means we have this hour to scope out those in attendance and see where they stand. The music ends and Albot leads me towards the refreshment station, the two of us taking a glass of sparkling water from the Maid passing us before joining a group of wolves congregating by the fondu table.

"It's a shame no one has found where Princess Crystalline is." A woman with her blonde hair pulled into a bun wearing a black lace masks sighs out, shocking me as I come to stand beside her.

"Sorry to intrude, but what do you mean by this?" I ask, curiosity lacing my voice.

"What she means is Crystalline is the rightful Queen. No one in this circle likes Alexander, but he is our current ruler. We have to obey him." The man next to the blonde states with a grimace, throwing back the drink in his cup into his mouth before letting out a small growl.

"We would be better off having the Princess become Queen than have Alexander on the throne." He continues, the remaining three people agreeing with him.

"Does everyone at the ball also share the same thought?" Albot asks, pulling me closer to his side as the lone male of the group stares at me with a hint of greed in his eyes. I turn my head away from him, ignoring his gaze and focus on the other four wolves.

"Sadly no. Only the five of us believe this. The rest just follows Alexander because of one perk or another." The brunet with an elaborate blue masks states, a sigh following her words.

"What about you two? Where do you two stand?" She asks, directing her gaze to Albot and I. I smile, looking to my friend who nods at me, allowing me to answer.

"I think if she were here secretly, I would support her and help her claim her throne." This answer seems to surprise the five wolves, but quickly they agree to my statement. With this new information, Albot and I link the pack to not harm them. They support me even if they have no idea I am here.

With a grin one his face, Albot whisks me away as we walk around the ballroom, chatting with the guests and dancing when we needed time to plan and check in with our pack mates on the assassination mission. A loud chiming in the ballroom indicates eleven 'o'clock, and Butler Loki calls for everyone's attention. The music comes to a stop as the dancers and guest turn their attention to the entrance.

"Announcing his arrival, King Alexander Thorn." Loki calls out, his voice echoing around the room. The doors are opened once more and in a lavish suit with a cape draped around his body, Alexander steps into view, his crown glistening on his head. Beside him is Narin and my heart clenches. My ex-mate stands next to my enemy with a stony look, neither smiling nor frowning. This ball is about to get interesting now, with these two making their appearance.

Time for me to play "keep away" until midnight tolls.

Chapter 26 – Battle for the Throne

I watch from the corner of my eye as Alexander begins flirting with a she-wolf, the low cut of her ballgown already proving her intention to seduce someone here. It wouldn't surprise me if Alexander sneaks away for a few moments with her after the ceremony has ended, but she will not get that chance. With ten minutes till midnight, I plan to take Alexander down without hesitation.

Since their arrival, my pack has interceded Narin when he has made his rounds around the ballroom, always stepping into his path to chat and ask about the possibility of joining the pack and becoming guards. This gave Albot and I a chance to avoid my ex, even giving us a moment to introduce ourselves to Alexander, with Albot taking the roll of Alpha of Astraea and me his mate. To think that man I called my father for eighteen years would be tricked by the charm to hide my identity and look at me with lust; a disgusting man like this does not deserve to live.

"Ladies and gentlemen." Speaking of that man, his voice carries across the ball room, demanding attention to him. I frown, placing my glass of water onto the table beside me as Albot takes my free hand. Now it begins.

"As you know, we have a pack that established itself in one year in attendance." Alexander begins, causing a ripple of curious looks to be pointing in our direction.

"Within that year they have shown a lot of promise and as such, I would like to invite them to become my ally. Alpha Albot, will you and your mate care to join me on stage?" Although it is stated as a question, we know that as guests we have no choice but to walk to the dais where Alexander has already made his way to, standing with what I assume is his benevolent smile. It takes everything in me not to rip off the charm and mask and reveal myself to this scum but we have to play along for now. Climbing the familiar steps, I feel Albot's hand clench mine tighter and look up to see him looking down at me, a grim smile on his face. I know how he feels. Whatever happens next will decide our fate.

"Hello, you two. Welcome to my home." Alexander states as soon as we stand before him, his eyes lingering on my body. I hold in the shiver of disgust and keep a blank look on my face.

[Everyone in place?] I ask, linking my pack mates in the room.

[Yes, Alpha. We are ready when you are!] Lilac answers, a hint of excitement in the Tracker's voice. I suppress the chuckle knowing how blood thirsty she can be, always itching for a fight. With a nod to Albot as Alexander continues his speech on tradition and howling at the moon in unity, I wait patiently for the moon to be directly above us. For the Question that is to come.

"Will the Alpha care to step forward and shift with me to complete the alliance?" Ah, there are those words. With that, I slowly take my ring off, Alexander too focused on his own task of taking off his mask while Narin steps forward. The moment his fingers move to take Alexander's cape I watch as my ex takes a deep breath and stiffens, his eyes darting towards me with shock and confusion.

"I will gladly step forward, Alexander, but instead I want your head." I chuckle darkly, stepping ahead of Albot and removing my own mask. I watch as the man before me also stares at me in surprise, his eyes darting to my prism-coloured eyes with a look of disbelief.

"H—How did you get in?" He stutters and I chuckle, opening my hand to reveal the ring that Cassandra had charmed for me.

"Hope this explains it. Cassandra send her regards in your death." I comment, passing the ring to Albot, who grins at me. I watch as anger contorts Alexander's face, the rage I used to be afraid of as a child now making me laugh. This man has no idea what true anger is.

"You have no right to my Throne. You aren't even my daughter!" Alexander bellows, the hushed voices of the crowd following suit as some question if what he says is true or if it's a way to try to intimidate me. I smile, slowly stepping towards Alexander and watch as he backs away and glaring at the silver mask in my hand.

"You're right. I am not your daughter." A collective gasp of shock from the crowd has me chuckling, making me stop my footsteps as the moonlight above illuminates me.

"I am Crystalline Thorn, the Lost Princess protected by Morai, Goddess of Destiny, and daughter of King Spirit and Goddess Luna." My voice carries around the room, over the silent crowd. Declaring my true heritage brings the power of a royal to my blood and with a smile I pull out the moonstone necklace from inside my gown and put it on, the orb glowing.

"I am the rightful Queen of the werewolf nation, and I challenge Alexander Thorn, my some-what great-nephew for my claim." My eyes never leaves Alexander, watching as his jaw clenches and unclenches. His eyes burn with hatred, and if looks could kill, I would be dead over and over again.

"The law states if someone with a claim to the throne challenges the current ruler, the current ruler has no choice but to agree." Albot exclaims after silence reigns over the room for a few moments, neither Alexander nor I willing to speak or back down. He knows he is cornered, that he has no choice but to accept.

"Fine. I accept the challenge." He grounds out through clenched teeth, passing his crown to Narin who stares at me with a look I can't comprehend.

"But it will be to the death. And if I win, your pack will be destroyed."

"Fine by me, Alexander. But if I win, your allies with be killed." With my agreement, I watch as Alexander shifts into wolf form without hesitation, charging at me with a loud snarl. Rolling my eyes, I dodge just in time to avoid his claws from tearing into me and shift. My dress explodes in a shredded mess of fabric, the remains littering the floor.

Shaking out my fur, I back away watching Alexander quickly spin around to face me and letting out another snarl. Giving him a low warning growl, I decide it is my turn to attack, bolting towards the grey wolf before me and slamming my small frame into him, forcing Alexander to stagger back and giving me an opening to claw at his face.

Before he can retaliate, I dart under his legs and to the left before whirling to face the wolf before me once more. Blood is seeping from Alexander's face, his left eye closed shut. Shaking his head, Alexander growls in pain and frustration before barreling towards me, a murderous aura surrounding him. Luckily, with my small stature I am able to jump just as he lunges at me, landing on his back and sinking my canines into his hip.

A loud roar of pain is let out from him, and before I know it, he has rolled over and I find myself being squished. With a yelp, I release his flesh and focus on kicking, my sharp claws digging past fur to flesh until the scent of blood grows stronger and the wolf above me jumps off in pain.

Before I can roll away, sharp teeth clamp around my leg as Alexander shakes his head, throwing me around like a ragdoll before releasing me. I go flying through the air, landing against the wall with a sickening thud and whimper. I most likely broke a rib, but I can't give up.

Standing to my paws, I glare at the grey wolf and push the pain I am feeling out of my mind. I am angry, furious that this man abused me all my life, that he cared so little of his mate and pup that he allowed Soulless to kill her—his mate and the she-wolf I called my mother. We glare at each other, growls filling the air between us, then I move.

Rushing towards the large grey wolf with the remaining strength I have put into finishing this wolf before me. He dodges just as I reach him, moving to the right but slips on the fabric that used to be my dress. I take this opportunity and spin on my back paws just in time to lunge and grab his jugular with my sharp teeth. We fall to the floor, him underneath me, trying to throw me off and forcing me to clamp down harder. I can taste the sharp tang of his blood, the red liquid spilling from the wound I am inflicting and dying my white fur with it.

His hind legs kick at me, scratching my stomach but I ignore the pain. Alexander needs to die. Shaking my head, I hear his whimper of pain as his jugular tears, blood flowing out faster. His kicks grow weaker until he is left barely moving.

Letting go of his flesh, I back away to see his eyes staring at me with shock, the wolf I once feared slowly dying in front of me. I want to let him suffer, left him feel the fear and pain many under his rule faced and then I remember the crowd around us. If I leave Alexander to suffer, I will be just like him even if we all know he deserves it.

With a sigh, I shift into my skin form and limp towards Alexander, letting him see me as my left hand turns to claws and I tear into his neck, reaching for his spinal cord. With one last look at the now-defeated King, I pull and snap his spine and kill him instantly.

Power seeps into my body, power that connects me to every wolf in my nation, power that awakens the Royal blood inside me, speeding up the healing process as my wounds from the fight instantly heal. I can hear the wolves of the Royal Pack through the pack link, many asking why they can no longer feel Alexander while others explain that I have killed him. I chuckle, turning to link my wolves only to find nothing. I try again, trying to link anyone in Astraea and look to Albot with panic.

"Can you link them?" I ask as he steps closer, wrapping his jacket around my naked body.

"Link who?" He asks, confused.

"Our pack! I can't link anyone in Astraea." Panic settles in and I wonder if the wolves I call my family have fallen into a trap.

"Crystalline, you defeated Alexander and are now the Queen. You lost the ability to link Astraea when you snapped his neck." Albot calmly explains, running his fingers through my messy hair as he pulls me into his arms. I take in his scent, forcing myself to calm down.

"So they are safe?" I ask quietly, burying my face into his chest.

"They are safe. Alexander and his followers are dead, and you are the Queen."

Chapter 27 – Narin's Truth

Sitting on my throne, I watch as the maids of the palace run about, happily chatting as they do their work. A week has passed since I killed Alexander, a week spent settling in the Royal Pack, weeding out traitors, and fully accepting those who bend the knee to me into the pack. Everything seems like a blur, from throwing traitors into dungeons to interrogating those who attended the ball to hosting a Zoom meeting with Alphas around the world to explain why Alexander was killed and my true identity.

"Crystalline." Albot calls out, his smile and soft gaze just for me as he approaches the throne, scooping me into his arms. The maids giggle, used to our displays of affection for one another as he has done this many times in this stressful week, the worst part being when a maid walked in on us kissing on the balcony after me having a breakdown from the stress of dealing with traitors.

"It's time, darling. You need to face him for us to be together." Albot whispers into my ear as he tucks my head under his chin. I close my eyes and take a deep breath, understanding what he means. After the ball, Narin was thrown into a cell for being the Beta. Although he is being held prisoner I made sure that no one abuses him, that his food, although bland, would be made with quality ingredients until I can find the time to talk to my ex-mate. To find a way to break the bond still humming between us so that I can be with Albot.

"Does it have to be now?" I ask, feeling Albot carry me away from the throne and out of the room.

"We have time now, so yes." Albot answers with a chuckle, kissing the top of my head. I groan, burying my face into the crook of his neck and deciding to stay silent. He is right, now is a good time with everything settled and the only worry we have left is tracking down my brother. Albot carries me down the winding hallways of the Palace, his footsteps echoing softly off of the hardwood floors and stone walls. As we grow closer to the dungeons, the mate bond hums inside me, and I shudder. I cannot wait to be rid of it soon. I am surprised when we reach the door to the spiralling staircase that will take us down to the cells and completely walk past it, instead ending up in front of a different door, one that leads into an unused office.

"I had the guards bring him here. I figured it would be easier to call for help if anything happens." Albot explains, setting me gently onto my feet and wrapping his arms around me. I take a deep breath, gently pulling away from Albot and turn to face the door. On the other side is Narin, the man I haven't seen in over three years. The man that bullied and belittled me most of my life. The man that rejected me.

With another deep breath, I place my hands on the door knob and turn, pushing the door inwards and looking inside to see Narin sitting on the sofa just a few feet away, his head down and an air of defeat surrounding him. My heart clenches at the sight of Narin, a slight feeling of sadness welling in my heart. I know it is the mate bond and so I push the feeling down and focus on putting an emotionless mask on my face.

"Good afternoon, Narin. I hope you were treated well while we weeded out traitors loyal to Alexander and Coro." I call out, taking measured steps towards the man while Albot stays close behind me.

"Crysta—I mean, your Majesty, the guards you placed outside my... room treated me fairly." Narin bolts from his seat, taking a step towards me only to stop from the warning growl Albot sends his way. I motion for him to sit while I took the opposite loveseat with Albot joining me, his arm wrapped around my waist protectively.

"I see you met your true mate, then." Narin chuckles, running his fingers through his hair. Confused, I look to Albot who looks back at me equally confused.

"What do you mean by true mate?" Albot asks, motioning for Narin to talk.

"What I mean is, Goddess Morai set up the rejection." Narin deadpans, picking up the glass of water in front of him and taking a long drink.

"I always knew I would be her Beta and help Crystalline take care of the pack as she rules. Honestly, we all thought Matrix would be her mate in the end with how close those two were growing up." Narin continues once he settles the glass back on the table. I stay silent, wanting to hear what he has to say, what Goddess Morai set up with him all those years ago.

"I have a mate, but she is in a coma. I learned this the night Crystalline shifted into her wolf form. I watched as she and Trix talked by the river, watched as her body crumpled in pain until she laid there as a white runt. I was scared for her, scared for what Alexander would do if he found out about her wolf form. I ended up rushing to my home and was about to pack a bag to take her and run away, to keep her safe until she can become Queen." He takes a deep breath and looks up, his eyes meeting mine and captivating my gaze.

"Next thing I knew, I was no longer in my room but standing in this large library with a little blonde girl reading from a large old leather book. The little girl looked up when she realized I was there and smiled at me. She told me about my mate, Hanna, that she will be in a coma, and can transfer a faux bond between Crystalline and I. All I have to do is reject you on your eighteenth birthday." I take a deep breath at his words, feeling the mate bond dim like a fading light the more Narin talks.

"Why would she do this?" I ask, catching the wolf before me off guard.

"Because she knew that for you to be Queen, you needed to leave the pack. She told me this mission would be easier for both of us if I treated you like shit, so I did. I spent five years keeping Alexander away from you and Trix when the two of you trained while also calling you horrible names." His eyes tear up as he takes a deep breath, taking the glass of water for a long sip as he collects himself before continuing.

"Then on your birthday, I rejected you. I felt the bond the moment I saw you in that dress. It felt so strong, so real, but I had to think of Hanna..." His voice cracks, tears falling from his face as Narin looks out the window to his right. Without thinking, I reach out and take his hand, trying to comfort him to the best of my abilities.

"I had to think of my mate in the coma back in her pack waiting for me. I rejected you as planned and you left. You grew and became stronger, learned things you would never learn stuck in this pack."

"Did you know who I am?" I ask, wanting to know if Narin knew I was the Lost Princess or not.

"I had a hunch. You see, Alexander can't have pups." He answers, confusing me even more.

"I remember Matrix saying something about him being sterile when you rejected me. My father also told me that Queen Clarice was barren as well." I muse, thinking back to my eighteenth birthday.

"Do you know why he can't have children?" I ask Narin.

"Because I placed a curse on Coro and his line when the truth of your disappearance came out." A voice calls out from the door, interrupting whatever Narin was going to say. Turning around in my seat, I see Cassandra walking into the room after thanking Lilac for leading her here.

"Congrats, Little One on becoming Queen." The witch beams, coming to join the three of us in the sitting area, taking the armchair situated between Narin and me.

"What do you mean you put a curse on my brother?" I ask, eyeing the witch suspiciously. It's weird to think someone who is a good witch could work with curses.

"Don't give me that look. I was mad and young back then. So, when the truth came out that Coro tried to have you killed and Morai intervened, I cursed Coro, saying his line would slowly die out and that by his one-hundredth descendant, no one will be able to have pups until you were found. Alexander turned out to be the one hundredth and you were found." The red-headed witch explains flippantly, leaning back into her seat as she chuckles.

"Hey wolf, how many whores did Alexander have?" She directs her attention to Narin, her question shocking all of us.

"Ten, I believe. I know their names and where they are." He answers, looking at me with shock.

"Better get them checked. It wouldn't surprise me if he managed to knock one up now that the curse is lifted." Speechless at her carefree words, I link the pack doctor to get the list of names of Alexander's consorts and order him to do a pregnancy test on them. If Alexander did manage to sire a pup, I will pay the she-wolf to give the pup to me and raise them to be a better wolf than their father.

"Look, you may not trust me, Crystalline, and I understand that, but believe me when I say I did what I had to do because Goddess Morai told me to." I see the sincerity in Narin's eyes, the sadness in their depth. With a sigh, I look to Albot who nods. What happens to Narin is my decision, and mine alone. I could banish this wolf from my pack, I could kill him, I could even strip him of his title of Beta and make him an Omega.

"I believe you, Narin. You only did what Morai asked, and when I meet this Goddess, I have a few choice words to tell her. But I won't punish you for what you did." I start, turning to face him. A look of hope radiates off of Narin, his tired eyes looking a little brighter as I continue.

"I need a Beta, a wolf who can help me and Albot with this pack as we plan to mate. If you can prove your loyalty, then that spot will stay yours." I state, seeing relief filling Narin's face.

"I promise you, Crystalline, I did everything in your best interest. I can even help you track down more of Alexander's and Coro's allies if you want. Just please, let me find my Hanna." His words are filled with the same hope in his eyes, and the doubt I had about Narin vanishes. Then there is a snap. Like a tight string was cut into two. Shocked, I close my eyes and search for what broke inside me, looking through all the bonds I have only to find one missing—the mate bond.

"It broke! It finally broke!" Narin cheers, laughing happily. My eyes open at this realization, just in time to watch Narin relax into his seat, his eyes closed.

"I can finally find my Hanna, and you and your true mate can be together." Narin mumbles, his body relaxing until silence settles between all of us. Confused, I look to Cassandra who silently rises from her seat to check on Narin, a look of relief on her face after checking his pulse.

"He's alive. The stress he has been under these years must have taken a toll on him. A couple of days of rest and he should be good." The witch states, motioning for Albot and I to follow her out of the room. I chuckle, grabbing the throw blanket resting on the seat behind Albot and I and gently place it over Narin's body. It seems every word he spoke is true, and I have a new ally in my pack. After linking the pack doctor to come check on Narin in a few hours, I leave the room with Albot and Cassandra, the three of us walking down the hallways in silence.

"So, I guess we have a Beta." Albot chuckles out as we reach the doors leading to the garden.

"I guess so. But I wonder what he means by true mate." I ponder, Cassandra looking at me with a smirk.

"You'll know soon enough. I have a feeling your true mate is closer than you think." She states mysteriously, causing me to feel even more confused than before.

Chapter 28 – A Declaration of War

I glare at the wolf who dares challenge my decision of preparing the safe rooms throughout the pack, the Head Warrior slowly shrinking back into his seat as he realizes that calling me a stupid little airhead was a mistake he could not afford.

"Marco, it seems your retirement is coming up in a few years, five if I am not mistaken." Narin speaks from my left, he too glaring at the wolf who challenged and insulted me.

"Th—That's right, Beta Narin." Marco stutters out, a look of relief on his face.

"Well, I think it should be earlier, with how you have served the pack the last one hundred years as head of the Guards. See Butler Loki now and inform him Her Grace has awarded you an early retirement. We can find your replacement later today." I chuckle, secretly fist bumping my friend under the table as he defends me, watching as two Guards lift Marco from his seat and escort him out. True to his word, Narin took over as Beta five days after our talk. He helped Albot create a list of supporters loyal to Coro and dispatched a group of Trackers to deal with them.

[Do we have a replacement candidate?] Albot links us, his hand squeezing my thigh.

[I was thinking that stoic Daniel you two have. He is fair when training and helps those having a hard time learn the new moves.] Narin answers. I agree, linking Daniel and telling him to meet me in my office later today. He would make a great Head Hunter and his mate would be perfect for training the she-wolves.

I frown at the thought of mates, wondering when my true mate will show up and praying that it is Albot. Every morning I wake in his arms, hoping for the bond to snap into place, only to have to hide my disappointment from him when nothing sparks between us. I want him and only him. Why couldn't Morai see that he is my destined mate, when my heart already knows it to be true?

"Your Grace, have you thought about my suggestion for training our soldiers for war? We cannot let their training falter or we might die when Prince Coro attacks." Lester, an advisor whose loyalty changes depending on who is sitting on the throne, states.

Bringing my attention back to the room, I frown at the man who still sports a light bruise on his cheek from the fight we had yesterday. This man challenged my authority during training, stating that only having training days every other day was not enough to protect the Royal Pack from Coro. He learned quickly just what my five-foot-nothing frame could do. I cannot wait to interview his replacement tomorrow and remove this weasel of a wolf from my council.

"I have, and we will keep the current training schedule. Just because there is a threat looming over us does not mean the wolves need to train everyday. If they do, they will become too exhausted to fight when my brother and his army comes." I state, watching Lester nod in acceptance. He knows his days are numbered after yesterday, and watching Marco being led out must have been his wake-up call to just how short his days remaining on the council are.

"Abbigail, how are the preparations for the emergency shelters going?" I ask the she-wolf, head of my maids. She smiles, her grey hair and thin body hiding the strength this she-wolf has. I personally have sparred with her since returning, learning a few new techniques from the three-hundred-year-old wolf who vowed her loyalty to me the moment she saw me at the masquerade ball.

"They are going well. We managed to clean out four of the six shelters completely and replace many of the furniture inside. Sadly, two of the shelters have fallen apart and are flooded from the snow. It seems they were not sealed properly when they were made." Abbigail answers, a smile on her face.

"Principle Lidia and I have also come up with an emergency drill for the students to follow in case of war starting unexpectedly and how to get into the shelter under the school. This involves the older pups helping guard the school while the pups ages five to thirteen make their way to the shelter first." She continues, impressing me. I thank the she-wolf, praising her hard work and for taking a concern off of my shoulders without realizing it. I catch Lester glaring at her and sigh internally. It seems this idiot does not like how Abbigail handles her tasks better than he can his own.

"Doctor Howard, what are the supplies like for the pack hospital?" I ask, the young wolf looking at me with shock before flipping through his notes.

"We have managed to get most of the supplies we needed in, but we need help finding a few herbs. I was wondering if you could get in contact with your uncle or someone from the Moon Goddess' Temple and see if they have a few, preferably ones we can replant and grow ourselves." The doctor answers. I find myself frowning again, reaching over the table to take the list that Doctor Howard holds out to me and scan the contents.

"I think Ira has a few herbs on this list. If anything, Cassandra has been moving back into her towers and should have a few as well. I will talk to the two tomorrow." My response seems to be the correct one as the doctor thanks me, even if he did give me another headache to worry about.

"Mom, trouble!" The door is burst open as Blake rushes in, his face a look of terror as he takes my left hand in his right and pulls me from my seat. Shocked and worried, I follow my pup with the council right behind me, the group rushing down the hall, past the ballroom and out to the front steps of palace. Soldiers in both human and wolf form stand there guarding the entrance as a sickly looking taupe wolf limps towards us, his head adorned with a silver crown made of thorns and brambles.

"How cruel, he never chose to become a Rogue or Soulless." Alice states, her small body standing at the foot of the stairs as she stares sadly at this Soulless making his way towards us. I make my way quickly to her side, putting Alice behind me while Narin and Albot take a spot to stand protectively in front of me. The Soulless continues to limp forward, ignoring the growls and threatening stance of my wolves, his eyes hollow looking as if the only thing that matters to him is moving forward.

"Let him through." I state, my Soldiers looking at me in confusion before bowing, creating a line on either side of the walk way. A spark of life seems to ignite in the Soulless but only for a second before the hollow look returns, the wolf neither attacking nor backing away from those that watch him, waiting for any signs of danger to end his sad life until he stops before me, bowing his head.

"State your business." Narin orders, eyeing the wolf suspiciously. The wolf growls slightly but drops a piece of paper he has kept between his teeth, ignoring Narin.

With another bow, he turns around and limps away only to collapse to the ground five steps into his retreat. The driveway is silent, all of us holding our breath as we look on at the Soulless, seeing is there is any trick.

Albot takes a step forward, looking back at me before turning to the wolf laying motionlessly on the ground. With quick strides, he kneels beside the taupe wolf, a sad look in his eyes as he looks to me.

"He's dead. The silver crown killed him." Albot stats, his fingers closing the wolf's eyes. I rush forward, bending down and gently remove the crown from the wolf's head, tears falling from my eyes.

Only one person would be this cruel, and he used a silver crown to send me a message.

"Find out who he is and send his ashes to his family. He never deserved this." I state, placing the crown on a pillow Lilac brings me before using my forearm to wipe away my tears.

"If he has no family, then spread his ashes with the rest of our pack's by the sacred tree." Doctor Howard steps forward, ordering a few soldiers to help carry the wolf away as Narin comes forward, the note this Soulless died to deliver to me in his hands.

"It's addressed to you." His lips are set in a grim line and with shaky hands, I take the note. Albot wraps his arms around me, pulling my back against his chest while I open the note.

Hello Little Sister

Congratulations on becoming Queen, it's too bad you only have a few weeks left to enjoy the power as I plan to take the throne from you soon. Be prepared, Little Sister, to give your head to me on a silver platter when the moonflowers bloom. Xoxo — your loving brother, Coro the Soulless King

P.S. I cannot wait to meet the newest pups in my bloodline, it's a shame that they have different mothers.

Chapter 29 – Realization

Sitting by the river where I first shifted, I think about the note, about the Soulless whose life was taken because of the cruel message my brother wanted to send to me. No wolf deserves to be nothing more than an instrument of war, a war that is beginning in just a few short weeks.

"Crystalline?" A voice calls out, the owner coming into view from the thick forest behind me. His eyes scan the area until landing on me, the wolf coming to the river bank and taking a seat beside my curled up frame.

"I needed a moment alone." I mumble, resting my head on my knees. Narin sighs, bringing me to his side for a hug as we watch the water tumble over the rocks below.

"Albot called Matrix. To think you created a pack and left that hyper wolf in charge to take over this place." He chuckles, a bubble of laughter escaping my lips.

"I always planned to take the Royal Pack. Astraea was just something I knew the wolf world needed. Matrix was trained with me as the next Theta when we lived here and I managed to slip in some Alpha training knowing that Alpha blood flowed through him." I explain, thinking about the pack I left behind—a place for those rejected and cast away to find a home and family who accepts them.

"Trix and Marcie will make an amazing Alpha pair. They just need a little time to adjust to it." I add, a small smile on my lips

"I bet they will. Matrix always had leadership skills. I knew he would be perfect as your head guard or take the Theta position back, but now I guess he will be too busy leading his own pack." Narin agrees, the two of us falling into silence for a moment. The wind brushes the leaves of the trees, bringing the scent of pine and oak, of fresh Canadian maple ready to be harvested for their sap.

"I found Hanna and her pack. I plan to go find her before Coro comes, to wake her from her coma and bring her home." Shocked by his confession,

I pull away from Narin to see the stoic look in his eyes. He is serious and I hate to break the news to him.

"The moonflowers bloom in two weeks." I whisper, looking towards the sky and holding back tears.

"What?" Narin asks in disbelief, his eyes staring holes into me.

"In two weeks the moonflowers in the meadow will bloom. That's when Coro will attack. You won't have time to get your Hanna and come back, Narin. I'm sorry." Tears spill from my eyes as I think about the night of the new moon in two weeks, the night all moonflowers bloom in the royal pack.

"I spent many years in that field to know when they bloom, not counting the hundreds of years spent in a stasis as an infant." I continue, wiping tears from my face as I break the news to my friend. There is a chance he may never meet his mate if we are not prepared. If Coro wins and takes the throne, then those loyal to me will be killed. Wolfkind as we know it will change.

"Then after we kill Coro, I will leave to find Hanna. But I am not leaving you until your brother is dead." His fingers pinch my chin gently, forcing me to look into those green eyes of his, full of gentleness. Something that I still find myself needing to get used to after years of his cold looks filled with annoyance or hatred.

"You will defeat him, Crystalline. Albot and I both believe in you." He continues, gently wiping the tears from my face.

"If training and putting procedures in place for the next two weeks before war and calling in our Allies is what I need to do, then I will do it." With that, he stands and gives me a smile.

"Can you also make sure that the two she-wolves carrying Alexander's pups are safe. We can't let Coro corrupt them." I plead, wanting to protect the innocent pups from the corruption of their ancestor.

"Of course. I can ask Ira to come pick them up and take them to the Temple until the war is over." He agrees instantly. I nod, happy with this idea as I let out a deep sigh. So much will happen but one thing's for sure, I do not want the pups Alexander managed to sire to be involved in this mess.

"You take some time to relax. I'll go call more of our Allies and have them here within the week." With that, Narin disappears the same way he came, his scent lingering for a moment before the wind carries it away. I smile sadly, returning to staring at the river as I think of the up coming battle.

We have two weeks to prepare, two weeks to train everyone together and gather our forces. I already fought for the throne once and won, now I will have to defend it from my cruel brother. I think about what I am fighting for, for whom I am fighting. I fought for myself, fought for the few wolves I call my family and for the pups I adopted before fighting for my birthright. But now what do I fight for.

Suddenly the calm of the forest with the scent of pine and maple brings in the realization that this is what I needed to fight for. The calm and peace. The wolves living their daily lives in a pack or surviving as Rogues searching for a place to call home.

The feeling of strong arms around me and the laughter of my pups sound just upstream and I smile. They are the ones I am fighting for. For pups like Blake and Alice who lost their childhood in a corrupt pack, for wolves like Albot sold to Hunters and forced to fight for their life in a rink every night.

That's when I feel it, slow tingles that start at the small of my back that rests against Albot's chest, the feel of a steady heartbeat synchronizing with mine and a scent that I know would send me to my knees.

A deep breath and a low possessive growl fills my ears as I feel myself being pressed tighter against Albot, a blush creeping up my face. The sparks are different from the ones I felt on my eighteenth birthday. Where those were a flicker of light, the ones I feel pressed against Albot are a burning passion mixed with a wave of calm reassurance.

I finally found him, the true mate everyone kept referring to when Narin spoke the truth. It is Albot, the man I have been praying to be mine every day since confessing our feelings to one another.

"Are you okay, darling? Narin said you were hiding here." His voice, rough with hidden passion, is whispered in my ear so low that only I can hear it.

"I was overwhelmed by earlier, but I am ready." I answer back, leaning into his touch and shivering when his lips kiss the sensitive spot on my neck.

"And what are you ready for, darling?" He whispers, his nose grazing my jawline forcing me to suppress a moan.

"To fight for our future."

Chapter 30 - True Mates

We watched as Blake and Alice enjoy the warm sunshine, splashing in the river while we relished in the mate bond surrounding us. We have waited weeks for this moment, for Albot and I to become mates. We were in no rush to complete the process just yet as there is so much else on our minds. We have time to claim each other, knowing neither of us would give up on the love that slowly grew over the years from our friendship.

"You two seem different." Alice says as she makes her way towards Albot and eyes us, her head tilted to the left as she looks at out bodies snuggled together.

"Different how?" I ask, smiling at my pup.

"Your auras, they blend together seamlessly now. Are you true mates?" She explains, her question surprising me. I knew the little girl held some sort of power, but to think it had grown so strong that she could distinguish mates together shocks me.

"Yes, Crystalline and I are true mates and the bond finally clicked into place." Albot chuckles, Alice blinking as she takes in his words.

"So I can call you dad now?" I laugh at how unfazed the little pup is, smiling as Albot nods and reaches out a hand to her, pulling Alice into the side of his body for a hug.

"Yes, Alice. You and Blake can call me dad." With that, the little girl smiles, snuggling close to Albot and I as Blake comes to sit beside our little huddle, a soft smile on his face.

"I never thought the day you saved us would give Alice and I a family. Thank you for that, mom." He whispers, leaning his head onto my shoulder. Closing my eyes and relishing in the feeling of my small family around me, I remind myself that this is what I am fighting for. That if I let my brother win the war for the throne, I will lose Albot, Blake, and Alice. I could not let that happen.

The four of us listen to the flowing river until Alice's stomach rumbles, reminding us we should head back to the palace and head for dinner. Blake chuckles, taking his sister's hand in his and heading back first. I go to follow, but Albot pulls me back to his side, his lips finding mine.

"Blake linked everyone that we are mates. No one will bother us here by the river." He mumbles against my ear when the kiss ends, causing a blush to creep along my cheeks.

His hands begin to explore my body, igniting a burning passion that crawls along my skin, setting me on fire and pooling in my lower abdomen that is begging for his touch. There is no words between us, just soft, passion-filled kisses that linger along one another's skin.

Our hands help to undress each other until I find myself naked, our clothes protecting me from the cold ground while Albot is above me, settled between my spread legs. I can feel his desire for me, his lips finding the sweet spot in the crook of my neck while his fingers trail down my body, over the curve of my now sensitive breasts and down to the one place that I have wanted him to touch.

With a gasp, I feel his fingers enter me, teasing me and enticing me into moving my hips. He groans, his lips claiming my own once more, tongue darting into my mouth to explore and taste me. My hands hold the man I love, with detailed tattoos along every inch of his skin, to my body as I ride his fingers. The fire inside me burns, the need for my true mate making me antsy to feel our bodies become one.

"Take me, please." I plead, pulling away just far enough to look into Albot's eyes and see the equalling burning passion in his deep brown eyes with love shining just as bright.

"Are you sure, darling?" He asks, his fingers slowing inside me, making me whimper.

"Yes. I've waited long enough, and so have you. Make me yours, Albot." With my consent, his fingers are pulled from deep inside me, another gasp forcing its way from my throat. Albot chuckles, bringing his three fingers still wet with my juices to his lips, sucking them clean.

"I can't wait to devour you every day." He groans, lowering his lips to mine where I taste myself on his tongue. My blush is a deep red by now, his erotic actions making me want more, want to be dominated just for a moment by my mate. I jolt slightly when I feel the tip of his cock against my wet lips, moaning when he slowly rubs himself against me.

"Please, just take me." I whimper, Albot chuckling while he kisses down to the crook of my neck. Without warning, he thrusts, his cock plunging into me hard and fast. The pain I feel from him claiming me, taking my virginity, bring tears to my eyes and I cling to Albot harder, my nails digging into his shoulder while my legs wrap around his waist.

"The hard part is over, darling, let me know when you are ready for me to move." He mumbles into my skin, kissing the spot he always favoured, the spot I know will soon sport his mark. The pain begins to ebb as I grow used to his size and I find myself wanting more, wanting the burning passion to build until I am consumed by Albot. With slow movements, I slowly grind my hips, moaning as I feel my walls press against my mate's cock.

"I guess you are ready." Albot groans, his hips moving in rhythm with my own. I gasp at the new sensation, my head tilting back and eyes closing. The pleasure and bliss I feel from our bodied moving as one with the sparks and flames of the mate bond fueling our instincts leaves me speechless, unable to form words and can only voice my pleasure with moans, whimpers and mewls of pleasure.

I feel the pressure inside me build, feel the need of wanting to claim my mate taking over as my fangs extend. As if sensing this, Albot's hand finds the back of my head and directs my lips to the crook of his neck I always burry my face in, his fangs skimming my own and forcing a shiver of pleasure from me.

I start to lick and kiss his skin, the salty taste of his sweat lingering on my tongue as his movements become erratic, his body pressing hard onto mine as Albot takes control of our mating. I find myself unable to move, only able to ride the wave of pleasure while finding the right spot to mark him, to claim him as mine until finally I feel my walls clenching, a feral growl releasing from deep within Albot who sinks his teeth into me.

I gasp, my body feeling no pain but instead a spread of warmth from both the Marking and from deep inside me where he has buried his cock in my twitching walls.

With instinct guiding me, my fangs sink into his flesh and the taste of his blood enters my mouth. I feel our bond strengthening, linking us together as one for all eternity.

I feel complete, like nothing in this world will take me down with this man by my side.

After a moment of silence, with nothing but our heavy breathing between us, I feel my fangs retract, his neck now sporting my mark for all to see. I smile, turning to see Albot looking at me with such overwhelming love and devotion. My energy now spent, I close my eyes and fall asleep safe and secured in my mate's arms.

Chapter 31 – Allies' Arrival

The scent of my mate wrapped around me is something I have yet to get used to as Albot and I find ourselves once again in the council room. Everyone now knows he is my mate, seeing as four days have passed since we claimed each other. Four days spent finding a moment hidden away in the shadows of the palace halls just for the two of us between training, planning, and preparing for the war that is to come.

I proudly sport my mark, wearing necklines that reveals I am taken for all to see. Suppressing a yawn, I focus on what Lester is saying, how the Guards, Warriors and Soldiers are training under Daniel. I smile at the pack mate of mine, happy that he took the position when offered it.

"I have some news of our allies." Narin sighs out once Lester finishes. Today is an update on which packs being able to fight with us and their estimated arrival to the palace as well as which packs are unable to send aid, having to rebuild their own packs from Soulless attacks. Coro is doing his best to sabotage me. To prevent any allies from coming to help take him down.

"Dominic and Ariven said their respective packs will be joining us. There arrival is estimated to be within a few days. Matrix already said Pack Astraea are on their way as well, the wolves there wanting to help their former Alpha in ridding the world of Coro." Pride swells inside me knowing that Astraea is willing to still fight, even if we are no longer pack mates. Blood Moon and Silver Crystal Crescent have wanted to kill Coro for over five years now. With this war coming, neither will miss the chance to rip him and his wolves to shred.

"Any other packs?" I ask, clutching Albot's hand under the table.

"Geminie says she knows one that might help. I think it is her old pack Hidden Claws. Their Alpha, Lace, says she owes Geminie a favour, and her Beta Mika agrees." Narin answers, a smile on his face.

"Lace and Mika are good wolves. They were misguided by the previous Betas that were under Coro's control, but the siblings have proven to want to change the bad reputation the Blakes caused." He continues and I chuckle.

"I know they are good wolves. Geminie went to Lace's wedding last year. I am excited to meet them." I retort, leaning my head on Albot's shoulder. The meeting continues, Narin giving a tally on how many wolves will fight per pack and how may in our own pack are ready in case of a surprise attack by Coro.

Abbigail is next, her excitement lifting the mood of this sombre meeting. She starts by explaining the status of the safe rooms, the supplies per room and how everything is now ready. This information lifts a weight off of my shoulder, knowing that there is a safe place for my pack members who are unable to fight.

With this, the meeting ends on a good note and everyone but Narin, Albot, and I leave the room.

"Do you think we can win this war?" Narin asks after a moment of silence passes between us.

"With Bloodmoon, Astraea, and Silver Crystal Crescent yes. Add on Hidden Claws as well as our own wolves, and we will be unstoppable." I answer quietly, a smirk on my face. Everything is falling into place. The strongest packs are our allies, the wolves that I have trained with for years now coming to my aid, even if they also have their own motives for wanting my brother dead.

Suddenly, the doors to the council room are thrown open, causing the three of us to go into alert mode and jump to our feet. Ready to fight off any intruders, I take a step towards the doors, only to see two familiar faces, one with hair as red as fire and the other with hair that reflects light like a prism.

"You two are so lucky I didn't tear you apart." I groan, relaxing when I realize it is only Geminie and Amberle. The two girls laugh, taking the few steps needed to close the distance between us and wrap me in a group hug.

"Blame Amberle, she thought it would be fun just bursting in." Dominic retorts, rolling his eyes as he comes up beside the table, Ariven chuckling at his mate's behavior.

"Why does that not surprise me?" Albot sighs, moving to where his two friends stand to give them each a hug. The girls and I pull away, their eyes zeroing in on the mark on my neck before they turn their attention to Albot's neck where a similar mark resides.

"Crystalline, do you have something to tell us?" Amberle asks, her tone the same one she uses when one of her twins gets into something.

"Not really." I chuckle, wanting to annoy the older she-wolf. Her eyes snap back to mine as she gives me a pointed look. I smile innocently at her, Geminie backing away as she notices the playfulness in my demeanor.

"Hmm really, because someone is sporting a fresh mark on her neck." Dominic and Ariven chuckle at her remark, keeping silent as they watch this interaction play on.

"Oh, this!" I feign surprise, pointing to my mark as I see annoyance growing in my friend.

"Albot and I are actually true mates. So we mated when the bond kicked in," I continue with my nonchalant attitude. Amberle growls in annoyance, causing Geminie and I to chuckle. Of course I will pay for this when we spar in training later, but annoying someone I consider a sister is refreshing after days of dealing with readying my pack for war.

[Queen Crystalline, there are two visiting Alphas looking to form an alliance with you and aid you in the war.] Lilac links me. I frown, mentioning this news to everyone in the room, then exit the council room with the other five wolves following me.

[Tell them I am on my way.] I reply to Lilac. The walk is quick, the six of us reaching the throne room within a few minutes where I see Blake and Alice peering in, their curiosity getting the better of them.

"Mom never told us she had guests today." Blake states to Alice, not realizing I can hear them.

"Two of those people look like Matrix and Marcie. But we left them in Astraea." Alice adds, her head tilting to the side. She is right, and as I take a look at a pair of mates cuddling by the large bay window, excitement builds inside me and I rush past my pups.

"Marcie!" I call out, happy to see the Latina again. She turns around at the sound of her name, her face breaking into a grin as she leaves Matrix's arms and brings me in for a hug.

"Girl, I missed you! Being a Luna is hard work." Is the first thing she says, making me chuckle. I realizes now that something is different about her and look down to her stomach.

"You're with pup?" I ask, shocked.

"How the hell do you know this? I haven't told anyone." She asks in disbelief and I smile, breathing in her scent.

"Your scent is sweeter, and there is something mixing in with it that I can't put my finger on... A sign you are pregnant." I answer, Marcie grumbling about stupid royal blood and the stupid power behind it. Matrix chuckles, coming forward to wrap his arms around me in a hug before turning to his mate and pulling her to his side.

"I told you Crysta would know right away. You owe me fifty bucks." He whispers, kissing Marcie's cheek as he looks at her lovingly. Happy for my friends, I turn to the remaining two wolves who have watched this interaction with Geminie, Amberle and their mates.

"Sorry about that, I am Crystalline Thorn." Walking to the two wolves, I stretch out my hand and the blonde she-wolf takes it.

"Lace Alibaster, Alpha of Hidden Claws. This is my brother, Mika." Lace introduces herself, Mika coming forward to shake my hand. I take in the wolf before me, finally getting a glimpse of Geminie's ex-mate that rejected her.

"I was told you two were coming to assist in the war." I state, keeping my tone neutral as I get a feel for the Alibaster siblings.

"Yes. Sorry we didn't send a formal notice, but Geminie explained the situation to us. We owe her as well, as we have our own motives." Lace states, her honesty refreshing. I have a feeling she is a no-nonsense Alpha that rules just and fairly.

"What is the other motive?" Albot asks, wrapping his arm around my waist.

"We want to kill Coro." I look at Mika, the hatred inside of his eyes radiating off of him as he mentions my brother. To think other than Geminie and I, someone else would hate him as much as we do.

"Why do you want him dead?" I can't help but ask, curiosity getting the better of me.

"At the time I didn't know it, but the Blakes had a deal with Coro and he ruled our pack from the shadows. Gem was the one who forced our eyes open and made Lace and I realize we needed to change in order for Hidden Claws to succeed." He answers, his angry eyes turning sad as he looks down embarrassed. I turn to look at Geminie who just smiles at me. I know the story of her rejection, how Mika and the Blakes treated her. The rejection that followed and the pain she went through to be where she is today.

I also know she doesn't blame or hate Mika and Lace. They changed for the better and became good friends and allies to her. If she approves of them, then I have no reason to turn the two away.

"I will have someone settle your wolves in and we can throw a welcoming feast for both Hidden Claws and Astraea." I state, getting a surprised look from the Alibaster siblings.

"Tomorrow, the four of us can discus an alliance and sign a quick treaty."

"The four of us?" Lace asks confused.

"Albot is my mate and will be crowned Alpha King after the war. Of course he will be present." I answer, snuggling into Albot's side. Lace smiles, nodding as she lets out a long sigh.

"I wish Kyle was here, but someone had to stay behind and lead our pack." With our group now including the siblings, we head towards the council room to discuss training with Blake and Alice joining us.

Chapter 32 – United

I smile, watching Geminie spar with Mika as the Future Moon Goddess throws him over her shoulder, the male wolf landing with a loud thud onto the ground. Lace and I stand off to the side, drinking water as we watch the wolves from Blood Moon, Astraea, Silver Crystal Crescent, Hidden Claws and the Royal Pack train with one another.

Some are focusing on hand-to-hand combat, some human form against wolves, and some fully in wolf form, their snarls filling the air while they rush to one another in a mix of fangs and claws. It amazes me with how easily each wolf was able to handle the change in training after the four packs came to help in the war four days ago.

At first we had issues, some wolves refusing to work with others while the Guards treated many of the females as weaker beings. Lace was the first to prove them wrong by taking down five males head on, leaving them a mess on the muddy ground and needing a night in the infirmary.

"Do you think we will win?" Lace asks, turning to face me with a slight frown.

"I do, Lace. We have more than enough wolves between the five packs." I answer honestly, pride swelling with how strong we have all grown. I think about the days I spent as a Rogue, spending summer between Silver Crystal Crescent, Blood Moon, and the Temple of the Moon Goddess.

Blake, Alice, Albot, and I spent our days in the warm sun with each pack, training and running around. When Marcie joined our band of misfits, she learned how a pack genuinely cares for one another. With the help of Geminie, Amberle, Dominic, and Ariven, I was able to grow and become stronger. With Ira, she taught me more about the history of the werewolf nation, of the way my people lived at war with Hunters. Every time I visit her, she would encourage me to touch the moonstone in the restricted area. But the timing never felt right.

"Gem and Amberle already knew you were the Lost Princess five years ago when they came to help Hidden Claws. At first it was hard to believe, but I am glad they trusted us with this information. It made the decision to become your ally when the time was right." Surprised, I look away from the blonde Alpha to watch the wolves. In three days, I have learned just how much of a good person Lace is, how she loves her pack, and respects her brother as her Beta. It made creating an ally agreement with her easy. But to know that she knew about me even before I learned the truth about my heritage and decided to put her trust in me long before we met makes me happy.

"I am glad you agreed to help. I don't know if we even have a fifty-percent chance to win this war with Coro. I always told everyone we would win, but I was never confident in my words until today." I close my eyes a soft smile on my face as I think about the future everyone will have without Coro in it, how many wolves and packs can grow stronger, how our nation can become stronger. There will be calmer days as we work towards removing Coro's wolves, to help the Soulless trapped in turmoil cross over and gain a chance to reincarnate. We just need to make it past Friday and win this war.

"I am glad that Hidden Claws can help turn the tide. We all deserve peace, you more than anyone. Let's win this war and heal our nation." Lace states, her passionate words having me opening my eyes to look at her. My smile grows, matching the wide grin she sports before we both set our water bottles down and head back into sparring. We will all need to be well-organized if we plan to win with no losses on our side.

◆◆◆

The ballroom is filled with easy conversation and bits of laughter. After four long days of training, Albot and I decide to surprise everyone with a feast. We only have six days before the moonflowers bloom and Coro arrives with his army. Everyone can use a night of food and relaxing.

"Thank you for doing this." Mika states, sipping wine from his glass. I smile at the wolf, feeling like his destiny is not over yet, that he will soon return to being an Alpha in no time and Lace will have to find his replacement.

"Everyone earned it. We can't just focus solely on training and tire ourselves out before the final battle." I state, leaning against the wall. He lets out a hum of agreement, looking over the wolves and letting out a sad sigh before turning to me.

"I haven't told Lace yet but I plan to go travelling after the war," He begins, piquing my interest. I turn to give Mika my full attention, happy to know that my hunch is right.

"Something inside me is itching to leave Hidden Claws and as someone who has travelled, do you have any advice?" I smile, thinking back to my days as a Rogue and taking a sip of my own wine before answering.

"The best advice I will give is e-mail or call an Alpha in advance if you wish to enter their territory. Some don't allow outsiders, while others are open to helping a wolf out in their travels. You may even spar with a few."

"Duly noted. I already talked to a few wolf packs I know personally and some have agreed to house me during my travels." Mika cuts in.

"If you travel to the human cities, just know that it is loud, smelly, and full of other beings. Your best bet is to keep a low profile and just act like a tourist." I add, getting a horrified look from Mika.

"Why would I go to human cities?" He nearly shouts and I chuckle, finding his outburst quite comical.

"Because you can learn a lot from humans, vampires, and witches, like I did." I state.

"Also, you never know where you will meet your mate. I saved Albot from a dog fighting ring led by Hunters in Toronto." I add before walking away in search of my mate. Walking around the ballroom, I watch as Alice runs around with the pups from the pack, Destiny and her little brother Aster, Esmerald, Saphira and Brent not to far behind, her smile so carefree that I can't wait for the day where I can watch her play with her younger siblings when Albot and I have our own.

Unsurprisingly, Blake is in a heated debate with wolves from the other packs, my pup always looking to learn anything new. To think that three years ago they were scared of new people, never trusting anyone. Now, they have come so far from their past that I want nothing more than to give them a better future. The only way to do that is to kill Coro in six days.

"Penny for your thoughts, darling?" Strong familiar arms wrap around me, bringing me back into a sturdy chest.

"Maybe." I smile out, turning to face Albot.

"Care to tell me what you were thinking about, my dear?"

"I was thinking, we win this war and give Blake and Alice some siblings." My answer surprises Albot, his eyes widening as he takes in my words.

"We can start that right now!" He growls possessively, scooping me into his arms while others watch on, laughing. Blushing, I hide my face in the crook of his neck, his quick strides taking us towards the exit.

"Albot, don't overdo it. We still need Crystalline to fight with us in a few days!" Amberle calls out, the room erupting into laughter. She is so dead when we train tomorrow morning.

Chapter 33 - A Sense of Normalcy

Throwing Amberle over my shoulder, I smile triumphantly as the fiery haired she-wolf lets out a wince. For the past two days of training and meetings, she has teased me about Albot and our mating, about how she expects to have her band of nieces and nephews grow soon after the war. This just has me fueled to want to kick her ass even more.

"Geez, Crysta, go easy on me." She groans, pushing herself into a sitting position as she eyes me.

"Are you going to stop teasing me?" I ask instead.

"And ruin my fun, nope."

"Then I guess you are going to have to get used to finally having your ass on the ground all the time." I shrug, getting a playful growl from the Alpha wolf in response. I roll my eyes, holding out my hand and helping Amberle to stand. Although I have been besting the she-wolf, I still sport a few scrapes and bruises myself from sparring with her.

"So, two days until the war." She sighs, looking at the still sparring wolves around us.

"Two days until I kill my brother." I add, closing my eyes and taking a deep breath. Training ends an hour later and as the wolves gather around for their final instructions, I commit their faces to memory. All these wolves came to fight with me. Came to defeat Coro and usher in a new peaceful era with my brother gone. And it is my job to make sure they all return alive.

With an agreement to have tomorrow as a day of final preparation and rest, I dismiss everyone before heading inside. Tonight, I just want some time with my family.

◆◆◆

"So, we are watching a movie and binging on junk food, right?" Geminie asks while barging into my room. I roll my eyes, chuckling at the fact that she too has a slight immunity to silver before returning to the table where all the snacks were placed out.

"Yes! Mom said we could watch Disney tonight." Alice answers, already in her pajamas and curled up on the armchair she claimed.

"Good. Let's start with *Moana* or *Brave*. No need to have a prince involved." Geminie suggests. Blake scrunches his nose, already rummaging through the movie list and landing on *Mulan*.

"Wouldn't this one be perfect considering the situation?" He asks, Amberle chuckling as she shoves a bar of chocolate in her mouth.

"I vote yes!" Alice agrees instantly, Amberle raising her hand in agreement as well. I shrug, not really caring what we watch since I just want to spend time with everyone here. After tomorrow, Marcie, Blake, Alice, Destiny, Aster, Saphira, Esmerald and Brent will be in the shelters while we go off to fight.

"I think *Mulan* is perfect. It even has a sequel we can watch." Marcie chimes in, already curled up in Matrix's lap with a plate of food in her hands.

"So, *Mulan* it is." Dominic chuckles, eyeing his mate as she looks at the chocolate cupcakes and hands one to her. I smile, realizing how lucky I am to have met so many wolves that genuinely care about me. The palace I once hated now is a home I adore because of these nine wolves in this room.

"Are we late?" A voice chimes in through the open door. Cassandra, Mika, and Lace soon comes into view, their own set of pajamas on as they make themselves at home. Make that eleven wolves and one witch.

"No, we just decided on *Mulan*." Blake answers, Mika nodding in agreement as he sits next to my pup with Alice pointing to the other armchair beside her for Lace. With everyone now here and the night just beginning, Albot and I take the only remaining loveseat while Cassandra makes a bed of blankets and pillows to lay on. Just before the movie begins, a knock on the door sounds and I sigh, climbing from my comfortable seat to see who is showing up.

"Hey. I, uh, heard there was a movie night." Narin sheepishly says as I open the door. I chuckle and step aside, inviting my Beta to join us, which he happily accepts. With everyone finally settled and Narin comfortably sitting on the floor with Cassandra, movie night commences.

Chapter 34 – The Dawn of War

Standing in the throne room, in a white suit with a white cape draped over my shoulders, I look outside the window as worry settles in. The stars are still out, but as soon as the sun rises, all the moonflowers will bloom and the final battle in this war will begin.

"You okay, darling?" Albot asks, walking forward with a mug of what smells like peppermint tea in his hand. I take it from him, thanking my mate before taking a sip of the much-needed drink.

"I'm nervous." I sigh, leaning into his touch as he wraps his arms around me.

"I know. But we have been preparing for this moment, Crystalline. We will win this." Albot reassure me. Taking in his scent, I continue drinking the tea as we enjoy this final moment of calmness. Our scouts have already linked us that Coro is on the move, with an army of Rogues and Soulless following behind him. It is only a matter of time before we have to leave and meet him just outside the pack line in the moonflower meadow.

[Everyone is in formation. We are just waiting on you, Crystalline.] Narin links me, his voice calm. I smile, placing my empty mug on the table beside my throne and take Albot's hand.

"It's showtime." I state, his brown eyes hardening as he looks out the window.

"Promise me that no matter what happens, you will live." He pulls me against him, his gaze returning to look at me. I gulp, not knowing how to answer him. I have a duty to fight with my people. To see things through to the end. I can't just abandon them when things go wrong.

"Albot—" I start, only to be cut off.

"No, I know what you are going to say. But even if it's a lie, I need to know that you will promise me you will live." I see the worry in his eyes and smile softly at my mate, standing on my toes and pressing a soft kiss against his lips.

"I promise that I will do everything I can to make it back alive to you." I whisper when the kiss ends, feeling his arms tighten around me as he breathes in my scent.

"I promise to do the same too, darling." With this, he pulls away and takes my hand as the two of us walk towards the palace entrance. We can hear the soft chatter of our army, the wolves from our allies blending in with our pack, all dressed in black. Everyone has a somber face, their eyes filled with every emotion imaginable as they turn to salute me the moment I step onto the top step. Taken aback, I look to find Amberle, Dominic, Geminie, Ariven, Mika, Lace, and Narin standing at the front, my friends looking at me with hope and trust in their eyes.

[Make a speech.] Albot links me, squeezing my hand. I nod, taking in the faces of all the wolves once more before taking a deep breath.

"I first want to start with thanking everyone here for offering their assistance in this war. Know you all have different reasons for fighting, but we share the same end goal and for that, I thank you all." I say, feeling more confident with each word uttered.

"Today will be a long battle as we face Coro and his army of Rogues and Soulless. Normally, I would say that if they surrender, capture them. But today, we cannot show any mercy. These wolves showed no mercy to their victims for years. They have raped, killed, and stolen for Coro with no regard to anyone. Anyone who sides with Coro is the enemy today. We will send all who stands with Coro to the other side and let Goddess Lisandra decide their fate from there." Geminie nods in agreement, the Future Moon Goddess knowing that her mother has already agreed to this. The pool of reincarnation will be working hard after today, the souls repenting for the horrible deeds they have committed while under Coro's leadership.

"Finally, I ask that you consider your own life. I don't wish for anyone to die today, so be as ruthless as you can. You all have loved ones waiting for your safe return, I am waiting for your safe return. So fight like your life depends on it, until Coro is dead and his army defeated." Roars of cheering fill the air as the fighting spirit of these wolves is ignited, and I smile. With a nod to the leaders below, I take the lead and start the trek to the moonflower meadow. The sun will rise in an hour and then the white blooms will be dyed with the blood of our enemies.

Chapter 35 – The Final Battle

The sounds of muffled footsteps behind me both in wolf and human form reminds me that the final battle is only moments away. The sky is fading from the indigo of night to a darker blue, with hues of red, purple, and pink on the horizon.

[Remember to keep the link open to receive orders.] I hear Albot state through the open link, a resounding "Yes, sir" from the hundreds of wolves joining us in this battle replying back. I smile, already seeing how great a King Albot makes. Once this war is over, I can plan his coronation and then together we can plan a wedding.

It isn't long until we make it to the meadow, the flower buds still closed, waiting for the right time to bloom. I think back to the first time I met my father, watching the scene of my adoptive mother finding me in this very field, as well as the memories I have of the two of us running around and picking these flowers to decorate the palace halls.

Now, on the edge of the meadow, I can see Coro on the other side, his wolves—both Rogues, some still containing their sanity as well as some on the verge of turning Soulless, mixed with Soulless in various stages of their beast side taking over—spread out along the edge, the stench of filth and rot blowing towards us on the wind.

"Hello, Little Sister." Coro calls out with a cackle, his sky-blue eyes staring at me.

"Cut the crap, Coro. You know I do not view you as family." I retort, standing straighter and holding my head high. His smirk drops as he eyes me, and I can only imagine what is going through his mind.

"Whether you see me as family is of no relevance, Crystalline. We share the same blood." He flippantly says, waving his hand in a dismissive manner. I glare at him, not wanting to play into his word games. Suddenly, his eyes shift from me to the she-wolf standing to my right, a lust-filled look filling his face as he eyes Geminie.

"Ah, my Geminie. So nice to see you are doing well. Maybe I will let you live and take you as a mate after all this. A Queen with Royal Blood, even if diluted, will be perfect by my side." He taunts. Ariven shifts closer to his mate, a feral growl sounding through the meadow. We all know Coro raped Geminie as a child. He tried to force a mark on her five years ago. The question now is who will kill Coro first—me or Geminie.

[The moment the flowers bloom, all Trackers are to rush the weaker wolves. Focus on the Soulless on the verge of death. If you have to, work in pairs. Hunters, you go for the Rogues that are the strongest. Those are the ones who will be using their knowledge and not their instincts to fight.] I command, letting Coro continue to try and taunt us from the other side into starting the battle before the flowers have bloomed. But we know better.

[Can we slowly start to make our way around the forest? We can make it to them just in time for the flowers to bloom.] Scarlet, one of Amberle's Trackers, asks. I think over the question for a moment, looking to the sky to see the small rays of sunshine slowly starting to stretch across the sky. The flowers will bloom any moment now.

[Yes, but only those confident enough to stay as silent as the wind.] With that, I feel a shift as some wolves fade back. Trackers always amaze me with how ghostlike their movements are, rivalling my own. It would be easier for them to kill the Soulless and let their souls become whole again and rejoin the wolves on the other side. Maybe they could be reborn as sane wolves and find love and a better life.

[Those from the Royal Pack, you will help to kill the wolves that are the weakest. I know your speed, and it is just below that of the Trackers. Again, all of you, Hunters and Guards, can pair up if you see fit.] I continue the orders.

[If you see anything suspicious or need help, send it through the link.]

"Crystalline, this war will be over if you just hand me your crown." Coro's voice brings my attention back to him after the orders have been sent. I can see his cocky smile once again on his face as I scoff at his words. I will not give my Crown to him willingly.

"If you want my Crown so badly, then you will have to take it from my dead body." I shout back, letting out a low growl. I can see a flash of anger in his eyes as he stares at me, his cocky grin falling from his face.

"If that's how you want to play it, then so be it, Little Sister. Today, your short reign as Queen will come to an end, and I will kill you." His words are spoken angrily, his hatred for me felt through the air. But he has nothing to be angry about. Had he been a good older brother, we could have fought for the throne properly as pups. I could have lived in the era I was born in and grew up with my twin. But Coro brought this disaster upon us himself. Today, he will be the one to die.

Silence settles between the two sides, only the occasional growl and snarls filling the air. And then the sun rose and with it came the blooming of the moonflowers. Their white petals cover the ground in a blanket of floral scents. It's a shame that now their will be blood staining their purity.

"Attack, my soldiers, and bring me my sister's head!" Coro commands, a resounding scream coming from his wolves. This is all we need for my army to rush forward, the final battle now beginning.

Chapter 36 – Coro's End

The Trackers quickly descend from the trees surrounding the meadow, their agile bodies making quick work in slicing open their unsuspecting target's throat before they move on to the next. The Hunters have paired up with a Royal Soldier, taking turns attacking and defending the other as piles of dead Rogues fall to the ground.

All around me are furs of various colours. At one point, I catch sight of Amberle's fire-coloured wolf and Dominic's ice-coloured wolf ripping apart a black Soulless before they disappear once again. I know my white fur is an easier target, as I dodge and fight off multiple Soulless at a time.

I find myself in an endless cycle of dodge, claw, bite, kill, and retreat while leaving a trail of dead Soulless in my wake. My muzzle is now stained black by the foul blood of the decaying wolves, but sadly I have grown used to the stench since an hour of battling has already passed.

Witches begin popping in and taking the wolves from my side away to be treated. Thanks to Cassandra, her coven came last-minute, just in time to keep anyone fighting for me from dying to grievous wounds.

[Crystalline, go after Coro.] Amberle calls out through the link for all to hear, her wolf tackling down a Rogue that was just about to take a swipe at me.

[They are just trying to wear you down. Use your agility to dodge them all and go kill that bastard.] Ariven adds as the others agree with these two. I nod, knowing that everyone is right and that someone has to kill Coro for this battle to end.

[Go get him, Crystalline.] Geminie urges me on as she stands to the right electrocuting a few Soulless that have cornered her. I wince, watching as the dead Soulless fall to the ground crispier then when they cornered the Future Goddess. With a deep breath, I let out a long howl, the sounds of fighting pausing for a moment giving me a chance to see that my side is winning. Good.

Letting the power of my blood out, I focus my energy in finding Coro, allowing my Royal Blood to activate and seek out others with the same power inside. I can feel Geminie, her blood, although diluted, still holding the power of the Royals inside her. Then I feel his. Royal Blood with the foul taste of death and decay slams against my power, forcing a growl out of me.

For some reason, I feel like he is the cause of the Soulless and how they are created. Dodging the wolves in my way, I rush towards the source of this diseased power in search of my brother. Breaking through a blockade of Rogues, I come face to face with Coro and snarl at the black wolf with sky-blue eyes. My brother stands before me, his wolf triple my size, and I realize just how much of a disadvantage I may be at.

We stare at each other, sizing up one another while circling the small clearing of moonflowers untouched by the signs of war. Coro snarls a warning at me, his sharp canines dripping with saliva. I growl back, ready to dodge at a moments notice.

As if pulled by some unknown force, Coro and I lunge towards each other. His sharp canines are directed to my throat and I suppress a chuckle. How predictable of him to go right for the kill. With quick footwork, I twist my body around to his left side and drag my claws along his flank. He howls with pain, turning to snap at my hind leg but I leap out of the way and retreat to a safe distance. I am surprised to see black blood dripping from his wound, droplets falling onto the snow-white flowers causing them to instantly wither and die.

His blood must be the answer to the Soulless crisis.

Coro lets out a loud snarl, his sky-blue eyes slowly turning a bright red like the Soulless as anger radiates off of him. He is not happy with being injured by me. Too bad, though, because I plan to kill this bastard.

Without warning, I push off the ground and into the air, my claws outstretched and aiming for his neck. He retreats just in time for me to miss my mark but what he doesn't know is how quick I can be.

With a smirk, I land long enough to lunge forward, my jaw clamping onto his cheek and tearing away flesh. Blood oozes out of his wound as his blood-red eyes glow. He meets me head on, though, and soon claws tear apart my right ear in seconds. Then I feel his teeth sink into my shoulder, ripping away the flesh as I jump away just in time to avoid a broken shoulder.

My blood trickles from the wounds inflicted on me, the bright red blending into my white fur. I need to finish him off, and soon. The two of us soon become a blur of black and white, our teeth ripping into our skin, claws tearing apart any place we can sink into each other, and snarls of anger and dominance forcing the wolves battling around us to stop their fight to watch and see who will come up the winner. Coro manages to catch me off guard, his teeth grabbing the scruff of my neck and throw me five feet across our battleground. My body lands on the hard ground, the air forced from my lungs as the scent of moonflowers fill my nose.

Climbing to my feet, the sounds of bones shifting and rearranging catch my attention and I turn to see Coro standing in front of me.

"Shift, Little Sister. This fight isn't over." He yells out racing towards me. I growl, dodging to the right to avoid his punch and shift. He turns on his feet fast using the momentum of his turn to land a kick but I quickly drop to the ground, my legs swiping his out from under him. His face holds a look of shock as he crashes to the ground with a loud thud and I smirk. He may be taller than me, but being small means I am faster.

Before I let Coro regain his bearings, I climb on top of him, landing punch after punch to his body. The satisfying crunch of bones against my next punch makes me happy. Suddenly, claws dig into my hip making me wince from the pain and missing a punch.

My mistake is fatal as I am thrown off of Coro and hit the ground on my back hard, the air once again being force from my lungs. Coro is quick to climb on top of me, His hands wrapping around my throat before I can take a breath of air.

"This it the end for you, Little Sister." His voice is filled with triumph as his grip tightens and black dots fill my vision. I know both of us are on our last stand. With determination, one hand grasps Coro's neck while the other reaches towards his chest as I dig my claws into him. I hear his pained gasps as he tries his best to strangle me.

With my body deprived of the precious oxygen that I need, I dig and search for his heart, surprised to know it is still beating.

My clawed hand clasps the organ tightly, feeling the heart beating against my skin. He growls, wincing while tightening his hold on me. My vision starts to fade, my strength leaving with it. With the last ounce of power inside me I have left, I pull my hand back and as darkness takes over my vision I pray to the Moon Goddess that I have finally killed Coro.

Chapter 37 – The Royal Family

Bright light forces the darkness to fade, and I find myself standing in the field of moonflowers I had just fought in. There is no signs of war before me, and I wonder if what happened was a dream.

"I see you are awake." A voice I have longed to hear once more calls out. Turning around, I find my father leaning against a tree, his eyes filled with warmth. I rush to his side, my father pushing off from the tree to catch me in his arms as he hugs me tightly to him. The scent of the moon is on him and I smile, feeling the comforting embrace of a parent calm me.

"You did good, my pup. I am proud of you." He whispers, stroking my hair. All I can do is nod, my voice constricted as I allow the tears to flow down my face.

"Am I dead?" I finally am able to ask after some time has passed.

"No. You are just in the dream-scape right now as your body heals. Now you have some people that want to meet you." My father answers, pulling away from me. The scene changes in a blur and I look around watching the trees shift from coniferous trees to deciduous. The blurry scene soon becomes clear and I am no longer in the moonflower meadow.

"Where are we now?" I ask confusion laced in my voice. In the distance a mansion log cabin sits by a lake and wolves lay lazily about, keeping their eyes on us. One wolf in particular catches my eyes—a she-wolf with long, flowing, pure white hair with a slight iridescent sheen to it. In her arms is a newborn wrapped in a white blanket, his black hair short and fuzzy as he sleeps in her embrace.

My father says nothing but places his hand on the small of my back and leads me to the woman. As I grow closer, I can see the shimmer of tears on her face, her prism-like eyes looking over me before turning to look at my father.

"Spirit, is this our Crystalline?" She asks, holding back sobs.

"It is, Luna. Our daughter is here for a visit." Father answers her, his voice soft as he looks down at me. Tears flow in my own eyes as I take in my mother, my true mother. How I wondered what she looked like and if I took after her in any way; it seems I have her eyes.

"Grand Mother, let me hold the pup." A woman speaks up, walking over and taking the baby in my mother's arms. My father pushes me forward and the scent of moonflowers and magic wraps around me while soft arms that I used to dream of hold me tight. Tears spill once again and I take in my mother's scent, not wanting this moment to end.

"Mother, where am I?" I ask through sobs as we are reunited for the first time in centuries.

"You're in the domain of the Royal Court." She answers, pulling away to caress my face.

"You and Selene look so much alike." She sighs, a soft smile on her lips.

"Am I stuck here?" I ask, getting a chuckle in response from those around me.

"Unfortunately for us, Sister, you will have to return to your body. Your soul was called here as Morai allowed us to meet with you." Turning to the sound of a voice so similar to mine, I find myself face to face with what I can only describe as a clone of me. He hair is just like Geminie, shimmering in the light as if filtering through a prism on a white wall with pure white eyes that hold a hint of mischief.

"Selene?" I ask, unsure if what I am seeing is true.

"It's so finally nice to meet my other half." She sobs out, rushing to join in the hug. Sandwiched between her and our mother's embrace, I bask in the glow of love I have always wanted.

To finally meet the twin I lost long ago and the mother whose arms I was ripped out of made my heart burst with happiness. I soon learn that the lady who took the pup from my mother is Celeste, Selene's daughter and my niece. She became the third Moon Goddess and carried on the Moon Goddess legacy after Selene.

"Is this your pup?" I ask her, smiling down at the innocent baby in her arms. An awkward silence falls between the four wolves as my mother and father look at each other in apprehension before turning to me.

"This might sound strange, but the pup is Coro." Father states. Shocked, I back away from the pup, from Coro, the battle still fresh in my mind. He had done so many horrible things, how could he be alive.

"Don't be alarmed, Crystalline. Morai and the Goddess of Fate helped to erase his memories. As far as this pup knows, he has done nothing wrong. He will be raised as the youngest of the three of you and will spend his second life here helping the souls he hurt to cross over, under Lisandra's orders." Mother reassures me. I frown but turn and look at the pup to see that the scars of his life are gone. His eyes open and reveal white eyes similar to Selene and father. Gone are his sky-blue and blood-red eyes. He is nothing but a pure soul now.

"Will he gain a chance to be reincarnated?" I ask, wondering what the previous Goddesses have decided.

"No. Coro will become a member of the Moon Goddess' Court and do what is asked of him." Another voice calls out. Turning, I find Lisandra standing with Geminie beside her, my friend looking around just as curiously as I had.

"Please tell me you're not dead!" I exclaim, looking at Geminie who shrugs.

"Nope. After we rushed you to the royal infirmary, my necklace glowed and I was called into the dream scape. Mother brought me here to meet the other Royals." I sigh, relieved that Geminie had not died before rushing to my great-something niece and hugging her.

"So I am alive?" I ask, worried about my body.

"Alive and with Albot watching over you like a hawk, the last time I saw him. Everyone lived on our side." I smile, feeling proud that I lost not one wolf to the war. Everyone is alive, although most likely injured, and not only do I have a mate to return to but I have been given this chance to meet my family.

With Geminie now here, we are ushered towards the log cabin mansion where I am met by many wolves. Some are royals that took on the throne, knowing the truth of what Coro did, others were Goddesses that ruled the moon and helped the wolves on earth.

Three days passed in a blink of an eye, with Geminie popping in and out to give reports to those still waiting for me to awaken and reassuring them that I am alright and will return as soon as my body is healed enough. I had learned through her that I had been poisoned with Coro's blood and my own blood was using the power of the Moon to release Coro's poison from my body.

Apparently, I was on the verge of turning Soulless myself because of this blood, confirming my theory that his blood was the answer we had all been searching as to why the Soulless were created.

"Why can't I find Alexander here?" I ask my mother one day, watching her feed Coro a bottle.

"Because we have a separate realm for Royals that helped Coro destroy packs and create Soulless. Many are of course from Coro's bloodline, but some came from Selene's as well." She answers, placing my brother into a bassinet and asking Hara, my great-great-niece from Coro's bloodline to watch over him. She leads me out of the cabin and towards the water, where many of my family members are standing holding a moonflower in their hands as they all look at me with sad eyes. Something feels off, and I look to my mother for guidance.

"My brave girl, you did so good. I'm so proud of you." She starts, Father and Selene coming to stand with us.

"What is going on?" I ask, Selene resting her head on my shoulder, something that she has done a lot these last few days.

"It's time to say goodbye, Sister. Your body managed to remove all of the poisonous blood, and you need to return home now." Selene answers, taking a deep breath.

"Will I see you all again?" I ask, not wanting to leave my family again. Three days was not enough to get to know anyone, not enough to talk to them. But I don't have the power like Geminie to go into the dreamscape and see them.

"We will see each other again when it's your time to cross the Moon. You have important things back on earth to take care of." My father replies, a sad smile on his face as he holds back his own unshed tears. I sigh and look towards the lake as the wolves that are my family, my many nieces and nephews, wave goodbye to me before one by one, they disappear.

"I know. I have a nation to rule over and a mess to clean up." My reply comes and I turn to look at each of my family members one by one, committing them to memory, so that when the time comes and we are reunited, I can rush into their arms and spend eternity with them.

"Your something important, Sister, is the little one growing inside of you." Selene chuckles, poking my cheek. Shock and disbelief fills me as I look at my parents, silently asking them if what she said was true. They both nod, My mother wiping away tears as she looks at me with loving eyes.

"It's your turn to add to my grandchildren, young lady." My mother says enthusiastically, pulling me in for another hug. I couldn't believe what they were saying as the notion of being pregnant seems absurd. I had never gone into heat, so there could be no way I am pregnant. Besides my body was savagely beaten from the battle. How could any child survive the wounds Coro gave me?

"All answers will be revealed later. For now, our time is up." Spirit's voice breaks me away from my thoughts as I stare at my father, a proud smile on his lips. I can't help but be sad at the notion that I would not be able to see them again until it was time for me to pass away. I smile back at my father and nod as my mother pulls away from our hug, only for my father to pull me into his embrace.

"Now, close your eyes. When you wake up, you'll be home with everyone." He whispers, his fingers running through my hair and lulling me into sleep.

Chapter 38 - A Date with Destiny

I open my eyes to find myself in a room filled with books. Light filters in from above and I look to see an endless sky. Looking around confused, I wonder if my father sent my soul in the wrong place.

"Sorry, little wolf but I intervened for a moment." A childish voice has me turning to face a girl about fourteen years old as she carefully writes in an old leather-bound book. Her hand flies over the pages, her face filled with focus on her task and I wait silently for her to be finished. With the slam of her book closing, I take a few steps forward.

"Who are you?" I ask, watching the girl tentatively. Her violet eyes are soft and all-knowing, as if this girl is someone who has lived many adventures. She stares at me with a serene smile, her little body slowly walking towards me until we are standing just a foot apart. She takes in my appearance from head to toe.

"I'm glad I saved you as a baby. You deserve to live with how you saved everyone." She giggles as she takes my hand before leading me down the hall and past rows and rows of books. With astonishment, I turn to read every title I can, realizing they were names of wolves and other beings alike that have lived, with dates of their birth and death on the spines. All of these books are destinies lived and completed, and I itch to read just one.

"If you open them, your soul with be transported into the body of that destiny and whatever you do there, will change the book. So I advise you to stay away." The little girl states with a sly smile, her words keeping me far away from those books now.

"I haven't thanked you yet for saving the children, Alice and Blake. As I'm sure you've noticed, Alice has a gift. The truth is, I intervened when she was born. She should have died." The girl changes the topic, her body nearly tripping over a stack of nameless books before I pull her into my arms and I look her over for any injuries.

"Whoops, forgot those were there. Anyway, when I saved her I left a small amount of my power inside her. She's used it for the greater good, and for you to take care of her and her brother makes me proud." The answer to my question of how Alice obtained her power of reading and sensing auras is answered and I turn to stare once again at the teenage girl. A sense of familiarity fills me as I look at her, the girl continuing our journey to wherever she is taking me until we are in front of another field of moonflowers. Just inside sits a desk with two new books, their pages open to just the beginning. I want to read them, but the girl beside me keeps me from walking forward.

"If you haven't guessed who I am yet, I am the Goddess of Destiny, Morai." She says quietly, her violet eyes looking at me as her smile slowly fades.

"I always wanted to meet the little wolf pup I had saved all those years ago, and you are everything I hope you would live up to be. Crystalline, your destiny is not over and these two stories before me are a brand new beginning to your life. Take care of the little ones growing inside you, because I can't wait to read their destinies as they grow. You'll make an amazing mother." The Goddess smiles at me as she sits me in a chair. I had already known I am pregnant thanks to my sister, but to know that I am pregnant, and with twins at that, has me smiling. My hand unconsciously rests on my flat stomach, and the idea of it growing with mine and Albot's pups fills me with happiness.

Morai asks me to stay with her for some time before my soul returns to my body, the little Goddess wanting to get to know me. With tea now placed before us and a plate of cookies, we chat about everything from what paths I could have led on my destiny leading up until now, to why she chose that moment when my adoptive mother found me to release me from my stasis.

"The time just felt right. You had wolves who could train you and I felt Coro's power weaken. If I had woken you any earlier, he would have killed or corrupted you." She answers honestly before taking a sip of her third cup of tea. I mull her words over, realizing that she is right. Coro was centuries old, his blood creating Soulless to control in his army. He had weakened himself to a state where my own power could overcome him.

"What about Albot? What happened to us meeting now?" I decided to ask, thinking about my mate, who is probably worried sick about me right now.

"Albot was originally your soulmate when you two were first born. Unfortunately, he was killed by a Rogue just after you were kidnapped when he was just two years old. I kept his soul close to me until he could be reborn and the two of you could meet properly. Everything that happened was supposed to happen." She answers patiently, a mischievous smile on her lips. I want to ask more, to learn more about the destinies of others and how her role works, but after a sip of my own tea, dizziness takes over me.

"What's... What's happening?" I ask, placing my hand on top of my forehead as the room slightly tilts.

"It's time for you to return to your body, Little One. I will be watching over you, so do not worry." Once again, I grow drowsy, and a peaceful sleep soon welcomes me into its embrace before I can say goodbye to Morai.

Chapter 39 – Soul Returns Home

A soft, steady beeping mixed with the soft steady hum of another machine floats into my ears, waking me from the deep sleep I had been put under after my visit with Morai. I groan, not wanting to be disturbed and feeling sore all over my body. Opening my eyes to see where the noise is coming from, I wince and quickly close them due to the bright light overhead.

"Crystalline, you're awake!" Albot's voice, although rough and hoarse, fills my ears and a small smile plays at my lips. My mate is here, but he sounds tired. I feel his hand clasp mine and a kiss on my forehead leaving tingles where we touch. He is definitely still my mate. I try to say something, my mouth opening and closing, but no sound comes out. My throat is sore and dry, as if I haven't had a single drop of water in a long time.

[Lights are too bright, and I need a drink please.] I send to Albot through our link, squeezing his hand gently. There is so much I want to say to him about what happened after the war and where I went, but first I want to see him, to see the man who has been there for me for three years and who I love so much.

I feel his hand let go of mine and another kiss on my forehead before I feel his presence move away from my side. A small whimper leaves my dry throat and all I want is for him to be beside me again. A few minutes pass before Albot returns to my bedside, his hand once again taking mine as he places a kiss on my lips.

"You can open your eyes now, darling." Albot whispers, his voice sounding as if he is on the verge of tears. Slowly, my eyes peel open to be greeted by a dim room. Soft light from the lamp beside me is just enough to see that I am in the royal infirmary, my body in its own private room I know is reserved for the Alpha Queen and King. The beeping machine continues to beep at a steady pace and I turn to face a heart monitor next to an I.V., with the cord attached to my right arm. Finally I look to my left to see a weary Albot staring at me, a relieved smile on his face as tears fall from his eyes.

[Water, please.] I ask through our link, Albot nodding as he turns to the table on his right and brings a cup with a straw to my lips. I greedily drink in the cool liquid that quenches my dry throat, finishing two glasses before my throat feels better and not as dry as the Sahara Desert. With my third glass placed on the table beside a now empty water pitcher, Albot chuckles as I look longingly at the ice cold drink.

"You need to slow down on the water now, Crystalline. You haven't had anything in your stomach for a while, and I don't want you to puke up water." Albot chastises me with a relieved grin, scooting closer to the bed to hold my hand once again in his. The low amount of light does little to hide the exhaustion on his face and the shadow of a beard growing along his jaw. I frown and reach out to run my free hand along the stubble.

[Why haven't you slept?] I ask, doing my best to move to the side to make room on the bed, only to wince from the pain. Apparently my body is still wounded from the war with Coro, and I instantly regret trying to move at all.

"Because you have been in a coma for a week now." Albot sighs out, his words followed by a yawn.

"Even with Geminie giving us updates that you are safe with your family while your body heals, I've been so worried about you that I barely slept a few hours a day." His voice cracks as he answers me, small tears falling down his face as his head lowers to rest on my stomach. My heart aches at my mate's pain, my hand running through his messy hair to comfort him. He must have suffered knowing he couldn't reach me, couldn't wake me from my coma while I was off having fun with my family.

[I'm safe, baby, so please come here and cuddle with me.] I reassure him as best as I can, smiling gently at Albot as he straightens to look at me, his tears still falling from his eyes. Albot stands, his arms carefully lifting my small frame so as not to hurt me - even though I wince from the throbbing pain of my wounds - and moves me closer to the other side of the hospital bed.

He sets me down gently, making sure my I.V. and heart monitor are not tangled before climbing in beside me and pulling the blanket over us. His arms wrap around me with his head resting on top of mine as he takes deep breaths, inhaling my scent. The feeling of being safe and of being home in his arms washes over me as I yawn.

"Promise me you won't leave me." He whispers, his fingers running gently through my hair, causing me to grow drowsy.

"I promise we won't leave you." I manage to whisper, happy to be able to speak albeit a little croaky. I smile, thinking about the babies growing inside of me and how soon we will be a family of six.

"We?" He pulls away, looking down at me with confusion swirling in his eyes.

"Yes, we." I chuckle out, tilting my head up to kiss his chin.

"I'm pregnant." Albot looks at me in surprise before his emotions changes to one of extreme happiness, a gently smile on his face as his hand moves to rest on top of my stomach.

"We are having a pup?" He asks in disbelief, his forehead pressed against mine as he takes in my words.

"Correction, we are having twins." I confess, Albot pulling away to look at me with shock. I giggle, instantly regretting it when I wince from pain. Albot quickly calls in a nurse, explaining the situation of me being pregnant and the nurses go into a panic, calling in a pack doctor to run some tests while removing the pain medicine from my I.V. poll. I glare at my mate for making such a big deal and order the staff to secrecy. I did not want anyone else to know I am pregnant until I am ready to.

"There seems to be no damages caused by the battle to your pups and they are on track to being healthy little royals." The Doctor states, a smile on his face as he looks at me. I sigh with relief as Albot clings to my hand, his own relief clear on his face.

"I do want to keep you here for another week to make sure you heal properly. If by next Friday you are healing to my satisfaction and the pups are developing properly, then I will let you return to your Palace on bedrest." He continues. Knowing that if I heal properly I can return home to the Palace and see my friends makes me happy, as the doctor takes his leave.

Albot climbs back into bed with me, his hand on my stomach as he gets me up to date with what happened to the pack after the war. Many have been working hard to clean up the mess left in the moonflower meadow, Cassandra and her coven are taking part in the cleaning.

A nationwide hunt to kill Soulless as effectively and quickly as possible was issued by Ira at the Temple of the Moon Goddess to help send their souls to Lisandra for reincarnation.

I slowly start to explain what happened to me while I was in my coma, how my soul was called to the dream-scape and how my father took me to meet my family. I hesitated to explain what the fate of Coro will be but ultimately told Albot. He is my mate, my King, and as such he needs to know what I know. I promise to never keep secrets from him as long as it does not involve a gift.

As I get to the meeting with Morai, I let out a long yawn. My eyes feel heavy and I know that I am on the verge of sleep.

"You can tell me everything else later, darling." Albot chuckles, placing a soft kiss on my lips.

"But I want to tell you now." I yawn, rubbing my eyes.

"I know, but you are still healing. Why don't we get some sleep?" Albot suggests, running his fingers through my hair and soothing me. He is right, I am still healing and also pregnant. I need the sleep for my wounds to heal. With another yawn, I do my best to snuggle closer to Albot and take in his scent before closing my eyes and let sleep slowly take over. We can deal with everything when I am healed. The war is over, Coro is dead and will never reincarnate, and peace can finally settle in my nation.

Now I can focus on healing the damaged caused by Coro and raising my pups in a time of peace when they are born.

Chapter 40 – A New Destiny Set in Motion

"Mama, who will be Queen?" Turning away from the window as I wait for Albot's return, I look to find my daughters playing with their dolls by the thrones, their white hair resembling mine while each sport one brown eye like their father and one prismatic eye like me. Walking towards the twins, I crouch down to look at Arora who asked the question, slowly playing with her hair.

"Depends on who is fit for it." I answer, standing up straight and picking Arora up in my arms.

"Being a ruler isn't just about pretty dresses and golden tiaras... in our case, silver tiaras. We have to be fair and just rulers to the many packs. We have to solve problems and disputes before a war can start." I answer, gently tickling her sides as she lets out a giggle. I smile at my four-year-old pup, placing a kiss on her forehead as she giggles some more.

"I hear giggling." Albot's voice calls out, a squeal of surprise sounding from Nova as I confirm that she is held in the hands of her father. She must have tried to sneak away to the training grounds again, that pup always wanting to learn to fight with Narin and Ruby, the new Head Tracker of my pack. A golden crown sits atop my mate's head, his tailored suit fitted to his body, hiding the muscles that I know are under the fabric as he carries our squirming pup towards me and places a kiss on my lips.

"How was the trip? Did you make a new ally?" I ask, settling the squirming Arora down and watching as she joins her sister in sitting on the thrones, their small frames giggling as they watch their father and me.

"Yes, we did. Next time, I'm staying home with the pups, and you can go to the next meeting." I can sense the tone of *there's more to talk about later* in his voice, Albot sending me an annoyed look with a sigh. It's been four years since the war ended, with many packs quickly converting to our allies and a few rebels that have had to be squashed. I have a feeling the pack he went to was one whose Alpha was still a supporter of Alexander and his line, and Albot had to help take down the Alpha for a new one, one we can trust, to take over. The supporters of Coro and his line are evidently the one thing that worries me each day, with my pups' safety being the priority.

I watch as the twins slowly slink away towards their toys, a hint of mischief in their eyes as they sneak glances at their father. Of course, the two little ones would be planning something for their father since Albot has been away for four weeks now.

Strong arms pull me close, fingers capturing my chin, tilting my head to look back as lips claim mine in a long, slow kiss, one that leaves me breathless with a promise of more to come tonight.

"I've missed you." Albot whispers, his lips trailing my jaw and leaving sparks in their wake. My lips open, ready to respond when the cry from the bassinet just by the window sounds, causing me to chuckle.

"And, surprisingly, I've missed that too." Albot chuckles, a grin on his face as he gives my lips a quick peck before striding to the bassinet and lifting a crying Isaac out from within. Knowing the girls are safe, I walk to my mate, wrapping my arms around him from behind and listening to Albot as he soothes our son back to sleep.

"Narin came home yesterday. He finally found his mate, Hanna." I inform him as we watch Isaac sleep for a moment.

"I wanted to wait for you to return before we welcomed her into the pack." I whisper, my eyes turning to focus on the twins when I hear a crashing sound only for Nova to call out "I'm okay." Keeping up with these two can be a hassle even with the help of the nannies assigned to protect the twins.

"Good. It's about time that idiot came home. We need our Beta, and now that he's found his mate, we can grow stronger." I nod, smiling as I nuzzle closer to Albot, breathing in his scent.

If someone had told me all those years ago that making a wish on a shooting star would lead me here, as Queen of the werewolves with a mate, three biological pups, and two adopted pups, I would have laughed at them.

I was unwanted by so many in my pack, unloved and always the punching bag of the King. Even now, as a runt, many still question me. But with Albot by my side, we have managed to grow into a stronger pack and stronger nation.

"Crystalline, we're here." The doors to the throne room suddenly open, with Matrix walking into the room hand in hand with Marcie as their son Jacob rushes in, making a beeline to where the twins play. I roll my eyes at my best friend who makes himself at home sitting on the throne before Marcie drags him off and hits him upside the head.

Geminie and Amberle arrive next, the two she-wolves ushering there pups to play with the others, while Ariven and Dominic talk animatedly about sparring with each other once more.

"How the hell did you manage eighteen years with his annoying ass? I swear the next time we come here; I'm putting a sleeping drug in his coffee." I laugh at Marcie's irritation as she walks over to me, Matrix bounding over to Ariven and Dominic as the three Alphas start planning which day of our reunion to spar. Albot chuckles, rocking Isaac some more as he gives me a knowing look.

"The next game of "I Spy" Matrix starts and I'm gouging his eyes out." The fire-haired she-wolf states, causing me to one again laugh loudly. Albot settles the now-sleeping Isaac back in his bassinet, kissing my forehead before joining the three other men, Geminie sighing as she joins us.

"You think that's bad, Karaoke Fridays at the pack makes me question why I haven't strangled him yet." Marcie retorts with the rest of us bursting into laughter.

"Could be worse, Albot has a habit of nearly suffocating me when he spreads out in bed. Many times, I've woken up with his forearm across my neck and nearly strangling me." I shrug, the three Alpha females looking at me with shock.

"Has the party started?" Atticus asks as he walks into the room with his mate, Heidi. I rush over to my uncle, feeling him pull me into a hug as Heidi chuckles next to us. Cassandra rolls her eyes as she comes to poke my cheek, making my pull away from Atticus to give her a hug as well.

The two witches had become Aunts to me, their coven helping with creating stronger borders for many packs and keeping our secret from the humans. Without these two powerful witches at my side, I don't know what I would have done.

"Hey, mom, sorry we're late! Blake was getting his ass kicked by this she-wolf. Turns out, they are mates." Alice's voice filters in, the small pup now growing into herself as she strides confidently into the room. Her once long blonde hair is now a short pixie cut, as she finds it easier to maintain between training with Ruby and controlling her powers. Her wolf turned out to be blonde, and a runt at that, so speed and agility became her focused training after her shift.

"Was not!" Blake grumbles, his head tilted away from me but I still spot the black eye he now sports. Whoever his mate is definitely has my support if she can put his ass on the ground. I cannot wait to meet my future daughter-in-law.

"By the looks of that black eye, kiddo, I say she kicked your ass." Matrix comments, getting a chuckle out of everyone and an annoyed blush from Blake. Cassandra sighs and pulls Blake to her side, her hand glowing a comforting lavender as she slowly heals my pup. I feel blessed with my family now here, the room filled with laughter as we all make our way to the den with Isaac in my arms, his prism like eyes watching the world around us and having the other ladies coo over him.

The plan is to catch up and allow the pups to play together while we leave our duties aside and just spend the day as regular wolves. Being a Queen is a tough job, one that has taken four years to figure out as I fix the mess left behind from Alexander, but with everyone here and their support I know that the future is bright for the werewolf nation.

I link Narin, wanting to know if he and Hanna would like to join us, but they decline. Hanna and Narin just want to spend some alone time today, after the week of her following me around as my soon-to-be Beta female. I remind them where we will be if they change their minds, before linking the nannies that took Alex and Theo to the training grounds to see when they will return with the two pups.

[Theo wants to keep training. His blood is strong and he will make a great Guard one day.] Mira, one of the nannies answers back, making me chuckle.

[Alex is ready to come back, he wants to play with his cousins and friends.] Kira adds.

[Well, tell Theo he needs to come back now with his brother. We are doing a movie night.] I link the nannies. I sigh, thinking about the innocent pups Alexander sired. After the war ended, their mothers returned, both ready to give birth. Neither of them wanted to keep their pups and had wanted to use the unborn babies as leverage to Alexander's riches. They happily accepted my deal to pay them each one hundred thousand dollars as well as allow them to relocate to another pack once the pups were born. In the end, Albot and I ended up with a couple of newborn pups to raise before our own twins were born.

"Everything okay, Crysta?" Matrix asks as I refocus on the group.

"Yes. The nannies are bringing the boys over to play with the others." I answer, Marcie chuckling beside her mate.

"First Alice and Blake, then Alex and Theo. How many other pups do you plan to adopt?" She asks and I smile, looking up at Albot who smiles down at me.

"As many pups as Crystalline wants." He answers for me, leaning down to kiss my lips. I lean into his touch, careful not to squish Isaac between us before we all walk into the den. Albot takes our son from my hands just in time for me to be tackled by two rambunctious boys, their hair a mix of white and black.

"Are we really doing a movie night, Aunty?" Theo asks, his blue eyes looking up at me.

"Yes, we are. So why don't the two of you play with the other pups while we get everything ready." I answer, seeing the delight in their eyes. One day, I will tell them the truth. But for now, I will let them have their childhood, something Alexander never gave me.

Looking around the room and taking in everything from Matrix pissing Geminie off to Marcie in the middle of a debate with Amberle, I think about just how blessed I am.

With the Soulless population almost gone and the peace between the packs under my rule growing, there is nothing I need to worry about with my reign as Alpha Queen. I can focus on creating a world for those needing a second chance. I can build a world where being rejected does not mean the end for the rejected wolf whether male or female.

Everyone deserves a second chance, and that is the destiny, the legacy, I plan to leave behind for many generations to come.

Rejection is the beginning that opens up the door to unexpected love and a better life...

Acknowledgement

To my co-workers at Spirit Tree Estate Cidery, thank you for listening to me endlessly talk about my books. For always asking me how my writing is while I get my morning cup of coffee in me after only getting a few hours of sleep because I stayed up the night before to write.

Most importantly to my work-mom Cara, thank you for supporting me the moment you found out I write novels and encouraging me to focus on my dreams. Because of this, you made it as a cameo character in this novel.

Now time for a much needed nap because I spent 3 months writing, editing and promoting this book while working full time as a chef with all you wonderful [and crazy] people.

About the Author

Born and raised in Brampton Ontario - also known at "The Flower City"- Alana Dyer started her relationship with books on a "Hate/Hate" relationship as a child that quickly became a passion for reading as she found that novels can bring you places never seen before.

From finding her love of reading, Alana Dyer soon began writing little stories as a child, and in 2015 with the discovery of Wattpad, Alana started writing seriously with the hopes of one day publishing. Five years later after writing for a loyal fanbase, Alana debuted August 30th, 2020, on Amazon with her first full length novel "The Runaway Breeder".

Now in 2023, Alana Dyer has published 6 novels and two Novelettes under the pen name A. Dyer and spends her days writing, playing with her many pets and planning to expand the distributions of her books.

Rejection Series

Three she-wolves learn that life can take a turn for the worst and those who are supposed to love you can become your worst enemies. When the Moon Goddess and fate play a cruel card that shatters each of their hearts and a budding war is on the horizon can each one find their true strength that lie within and figure out just who is the mastermind in the war that will change the fate of the werewolf race?

Follow Amberle and her Full Moon Rejection in "Rejection on the Full Moon"

See if Geminie's soul mate regrets "Rejecting the Future Moon Goddess"

Can "Rejection to the Alpha King's Daughter" bring out the true Werewolf Queen in Crystalline

And will these girls be able to piece together the true Soulless Evil that hides behind his War?

Rejection on the Full Moon
Book 1

Soulless - werewolves who have turned rogue with no humanity left, giving in to their beastly urges.

Rejection - an act in which your soulmate rejects the mate bond, causing immense pain to the rejected.

These are the challenges Amberle Crest must overcome after becoming an outcast amongst the wolves her age due to an event outside of her control.

When her mate rejects her on her eighteenth birthday, Amberle realizes that living in a pack where the majority would rather use her as a slave than treat her as an equal is not worth the pain. She becomes the notorious wolf, Fire Foot, vowing that everyone would regret how they treated her, as she leaves her pack in the past.

Now a ghost forgotten by those that tormented her, Amberle does whatever it takes to survive as a lone wolf. A fateful day changes her lonely life to one full of happiness and hope—until ghosts from her own past call for aid in ridding their pack of the Soulless who threatens all wolf kind.

Faced with new friends, old foes, and the threat of a building army, will Amberle be able to fight the ghosts of her past to cherish the pack she has found or will an old mate claim her before a second chance mate can show her what being treasured by someone is all about?

Rejecting the Future Moon Goddess
Book 2

Soulless - werewolves who have turned rogue with no humanity left, giving in to their beastly urges.

Rejection - an act in which your soulmate rejects the mate bond, causing immense pain to the rejected.

Moon Goddess - the deity that created the werewolf race whom her creation worship

Omega - The lowest ranked wolf in the pack sometimes treated as nothing more than a slave or an object

These are the things Geminie Blake learns after being blamed for the tragic Deaths of her Alpha and Luna. With the pack turned against her and failing to shift as a wolf, Geminie faces challenges every day with the hope of one day gaining freedom or her mate saving her. But when her fated soul mate ends up being her ex-best friend and the son to the late Alpha and Luna rejects her, Geminie's life changes drastically.

Learning that she is not Geminie Blake - daughter to the Beta couple - but Geminie Starlite - daughter to the Moon Goddess and Future Moon Goddess herself - Geminie quickly faces the new challenges thrown her way as she navigates her wolf form and Goddess powers, creating a pack that rivals that of Blood Moon and building her life from scratch to one day take up the mantel as Moon Goddess becomes her priority.

Now, thriving and loving herself for who she is, Geminie forces the past behind her as she waits for her second chance at love. When her first mate requests help and aid from a threat created by Soulless and a potential Leader of the wolves that have lost their Humanity, Geminie is forced to face the wounds left unhealed and return to the place she called hell for eleven years of her life.

Will Geminie be able to overcome the scars left by years of abuse and find love once and for all, or will the panful wounds of her past and threat from the Leader of the army of Soulless ready to kill at a moments notice take the last bit of happiness this young Goddess has left.

Rejection to the Alpha King's Daughter
Book 3

Soulless - werewolves who have turned rogue with no humanity left, giving in to their beastly urges.

Rejection - an act in which your soulmate rejects the mate bond, causing immense pain to the rejected.

Moon Goddess - the deity that created the werewolf race whom her creation worship

Omega - The lowest ranked wolf in the pack sometimes treated as nothing more than a slave or an object

Alpha King/Queen - The rulers of the werewolf nation

Runt - The smallest of the wolf pack, usually ignored or bullied for being the smallest

Crystalline Thorn grows under the abuse by her father as she trains to take the throne one day and become the Alpha Queen, leader of every wolf in the werewolf nation. She dreams of the day when she meets her mate and be accepted as a strong Queen, especially since she is a runt.

But her dream is soon shattered when on the day of an Alliance her mate discovers her "weak" form and rejects her promptly leading to her father disowning her and her hopes to inherit the throne is dashed. But that is the least of her worries. Soon, with the help of Geminie and Amberle, Crystalline learns of a war that has been brewing for thousands of years, of a destiny that has been written in the stars by the original Moon Goddess - Luna - and the Goddess of Destiny - Morai - have placed upon her and her connection to the Lost Princess.

Will Crystalline be able to retrieve her throne?

Will she accept the mate that rejected her or chose the second chance mate?

Or will the weight of responsibility handed to her crush her entirely?

The Run

"*The cage doors are released and I open my sapphire coloured eyes, dashing out of the prison and into the forest.*

Seven days for the full moon to be blue.

Seven days from the starting line to the finish

Seven days, that's how long I had to make it to the lodge as an unmated female."

Legends of werewolves have gone back centuries. Always including the Moon Goddess and her blessing of soulmates to the beings she created. But the ugly truth is there is no such thing as soulmates. There is only The Run.

An event created centuries ago held twice a year during a blue moon where she-wolves run from their male counter parts. If they are captured, they are mated and marked, claimed by whoever captures them first.

No one is exempted from this event - not even Grace Harvest.

After being able to avoid attending the event since turning eighteen, Grace finds herself unable to find an excuse not to participate this time. With her last hope of remaining unmated until she can fall in love, she makes a bet with her Alpha. If she wins, he can no longer force wolves of his pack to participate in The Run and allow them to find love. If he wins, Grace will be mated, and her pack mates are forced to go no matter what.

But what will happen when she meets a golden haired wolf by the name Caden Wolfrain, who instantly captures her attention. Will she do all she can to win the bet, will Caden win her heart or will the secrets Caden keeps force her to cut ties with this golden haired wolf without a second thought no matter the heart break.

Books by the Author

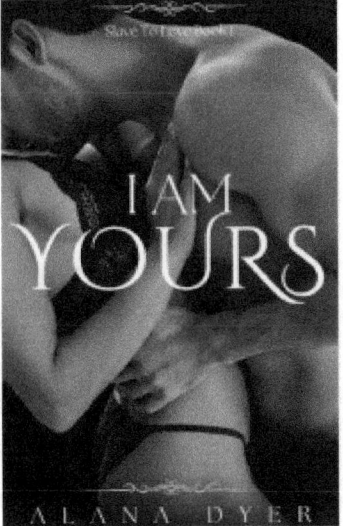

CONTACT THE AUTHOR

 alana.dyer.author@
hotmail.com

 author.alana.dyer

 alana.dyer

 Alana Dyer
@alana.dyer.author

E-BOOK | PAPERBACK | HARDCOVERS
available where books are sold

Don't miss out!

Visit the website below and you can sign up to receive emails whenever Alana Dyer publishes a new book. There's no charge and no obligation.

https://books2read.com/r/B-A-LXGX-OBOOC

BOOKS 2 READ

Connecting independent readers to independent writers.